1971

The Pineworth Chronicles, Volume 5

K.E.W.

Published by White Quill Writings, 2024.

1971

First edition. June 18, 2024.

ISBN: 979-8227150752

Written by K.E.W..

Also by K.E.W.

The Pineworth Chronicles
Secrets Among The Stones
1971

Standalone
The Pineworth Chronicles
Room Below The World
School Safety Pocket Handbook
A Walk Among Soldiers
Confessions Of The Lost

Watch for more at https://www.instagram.com/whitequillwritings/.

Table of Contents

To my wife, whose indefatigable support and love make every challenge easier to face. After all these beautiful years of marriage, your strength and kindness inspire me daily. Thank you for making this book and our life together possible. This book is for you.

Prologue

The year was 1971, and the sleepy town of Pineworth, nestled amidst the rolling hills and sprawling farmland of rural Georgia, seemed frozen in time. The streets, lined with quaint storefronts and weather-beaten houses, bore the scars of years gone by, each crack and crevice a testament to the town's storied past.

For Sam Anderson, a young cop with dreams as big as the endless Georgia sky, this was just another day in the life of a small-town lawman. But beneath the mundane surface, something was stirring in the sleepy town of Pineworth. Change was coming, whispered on the lips of the townsfolk and echoed in the halls of power.

As Sam patrolled the streets, his footsteps echoing in the stillness of the early morning, he couldn't shake the feeling that something momentous was on the horizon. The recent inauguration of a new Governor had sparked a wave of hope and optimism but also stirred up old resentments and fears.

The tension was palpable in the Anderson household. Sam's parents, products of a bygone era, viewed the changing tide with apprehension and skepticism. To them, the idea of ending segregation was nothing short of revolutionary, a seismic shift that threatened to upend the world they had always known.

But for Sam, the son of a proud lineage and a product of his upbringing, the winds of change carried with them a sense of possibility, of hope for a brighter future. He knew that the road ahead would be fraught with challenges and obstacles, but he was determined to face them head-on, to fight for what he believed was right, no matter the cost.

As the sun rose higher in the sky, casting long shadows across the sleepy streets of Pineworth, Sam knew that he stood on the precipice of history. The choices he made in the days and weeks to come would shape not only his destiny but the destiny of an entire town caught in the throes of a changing world.

Chapter 1
The Rising Light

The Anderson family home stood in the heart of Pineworth, Georgia, nestled among a canopy of towering pine trees. Weathered by years of Southern summers and winters, the two-story structure exuded a sense of warmth and familiarity. The porch, adorned with rocking chairs and a porch swing, creaked softly with each gentle sway, a testament to countless evenings spent watching the world go by.

As you approached the front door, freshly cut grass mingled with the fragrant aroma of magnolia blossoms, filling the air with a sweet, earthy perfume. The wooden door, weathered and worn, beckoned with the promise of warmth and comfort within.

Stepping into the living room, the senses were immediately enveloped in a cozy embrace. The soft glow of lamplight cast a warm ambiance, casting shadows that danced across the walls like old friends sharing secrets. The well-loved sofa, its cushions worn with use, welcomed you with open arms, inviting you to sink into its embrace and stay awhile.

The air was alive with the faint murmur of conversation, the sound of Sam's parents engaged in quiet dialogue. Their voices, filled with emotion and conviction, carried the weight of generations past, echoing through the room like a haunting melody.

In the corner, a crackling fire danced in the hearth, sending tendrils of warmth and light spiraling upwards toward the ceiling. The scent of burning wood mingled with the subtle aroma of cinnamon and cloves, creating a comforting symphony of smells that wrapped around you like a familiar blanket.

The living room in the Anderson household glowed softly, lit only by the flickering television screen. Officer Sam Anderson, a young cop with dreams of justice, sat next to his father, Ronnie, on the well-worn sofa. Governor Jimmy Carter's inauguration address on the screen sent tremors through their small Georgia town.

"The era of segregation is over," echoed from the TV, a declaration that reverberated in the quiet room. Ronnie Anderson, a solid pillar of tradition, shifted uncomfortably in his seat. Eleanor, Sam's mother, gasped audibly, her eyes wide with disbelief.

"I never thought I'd live to see the day a Governor would say something like that," Ronnie muttered, his voice heavy with disapproval. "Especially a Georgia Governor," he continued.

Eleanor shook her head, a mix of shock and disappointment etched across her features. "It's unsettling, Ron. It's just not right."

The weight of his parents' reactions pressed upon Sam, and he sat in silence, his gaze fixed on the TV screen. Governor Carter continued to speak, laying out a vision that challenged the very foundations of Pineworth.

"Pineworth is about to face a storm," Sam thought, glancing at his parents. "This town, clinging to its traditions, is in for a tumultuous ride."

Sam's mind buzzed with an internal dialogue as the governor's words unfolded. Pineworth, deeply entrenched in its ways, would resist change. "Can I really make a difference?" he wondered, grappling with the daunting prospect of challenging not only his community but his own family.

The living room became a sanctuary of charged emotions, the tension thick enough to cut with a knife. Sam, feeling the weight of the moment, rose above the silence. His gaze met his parents', a mix of determination and uncertainty in his eyes.

"But I became a cop for a reason," he reminded himself. To protect and serve justice. A fire ignited within him as he turned away from the TV, ready to face the challenges that lay ahead.

As Sam sat beside his father, the weight of their differing views hung heavily in the air. Ron's voice was firm, his words laced with the stubbornness of tradition. "I never thought I'd live to see the day a governor would say something like that," he muttered, his disapproval palpable.

Sam, his gaze fixed on the TV screen, couldn't hide the passion in his voice. "But Dad, times are changing. We can't keep holding on to the past. It's time for things to change," he pleaded, his words tinged with urgency.

Ronnie shook his head, his resolve unyielding. "Sam. It's just not right," he insisted, his voice tinged with frustration.

Sam's frustration bubbled to the surface. "But Dad, don't you see? We have to fight for what's right, even if it's hard. Even if it means challenging the way things have always been," he implored, his voice rising with conviction.

Ron's expression softened, but his tone remained resolute. "Son, I understand you want to make a difference, but sometimes change comes with consequences we can't predict," he cautioned, his words carrying the weight of years of experience.

Sam sighed, his frustration giving way to determination. "I know it won't be easy, Dad. But I have to try. I have to fight for what I believe in, no matter the cost," he declared, his voice steady with resolve. Their differing views hung between them like a heavy curtain, casting shadows over the room.

As Sam and his father engaged in their heated exchange, Eleanor, Sam's mother, couldn't hold back any longer. Her voice trembled with worry as she interjected into the conversation. "I wish you would quit the police force if there's going to be this many changes," she said, her words heavy with concern. "I worry for your life, Sam."

Sam turned to his mother, the concern etched deeply into her face, breaking his heart. "Mom, I know your worries, but I can't just walk away," he said, his voice softening with empathy. "I became a cop to protect, serve, and fight for justice. And right now, that means being a part of these changes, not stepping away from them."

Eleanor's eyes welled up with tears as she reached to grasp Sam's hand. "But Sam, I can't bear the thought of anything happening to you," she whispered, her voice choked with emotion.

Sam squeezed his mother's hand gently, the love and reassurance flowing through his touch.

"I'll be careful, Mom. I promise," he said, his voice filled with determination. "But I can't stand by and watch injustice unfold. I have to be a part of making things right, no matter the risks."

As Sam's mother wiped away her tears, his father's voice broke the heavy silence in the room. "But these are not your problems, Sam," he said, his tone tinged with frustration. "We've never harmed a person of color. We've treated them fairly."

Sam met his father's gaze, his eyes reflecting the weight of his convictions. "But Dad, it's not just about what we've done. It's about what we've allowed to happen," he countered, his voice steady with resolve. "We've been complicit in an inherently unfair system by staying silent, not challenging the status quo."

Ron's brow furrowed in thought, his gaze shifting between his son and wife. "I never saw it that way," he admitted, his voice softer now, tinged with uncertainty.

Turning to his mother, Sam sought her understanding. "Didn't you raise me to care about all human beings, Mom?" he asked, his voice pleading for validation.

Eleanor looked at him, her eyes shimmering with pride. "Yes, Sam," she said, her voice filled with unwavering conviction. "We raised you to believe in fairness and equality, to treat everyone with dignity and respect."

Sam's heart swelled with gratitude as he felt his parents' love and support wash over him. "Then you understand why I have to do this," he said, his voice filled with determination. "I can't sit idly by while injustice prevails. I have to stand up and fight for what's right, even if it means challenging the beliefs we've held for so long."

"We see things differently, son," he admitted, his tone softening with acceptance. "But that doesn't mean I won't be here to support you."

Sam felt a surge of gratitude wash over him as he met his father's gaze, a glimmer of hope shining in his eyes. "Thank you, Dad," he said, his voice filled with emotion. "That means more to me than you'll ever know."

Eleanor reached out to squeeze Sam's hand, her eyes filled with pride and love. "We may not always agree, Sam," she said, her voice gentle yet firm, "but we'll always be here for you, no matter what."

Sam smiled, his parents' warmth enveloping him like a comforting embrace. "I know," he said, his voice steady with conviction. "And I'll need you now more than ever."

With a sense of resolution settling over them, Sam rose from the sofa, a newfound sense of purpose propelling him forward. "I'm going out for a walk," he announced, his voice filled with determination. "I need some fresh air, some time to clear my head."

Ronnie and Eleanor exchanged a knowing glance, their silent support speaking volumes. "Take your time, Sam," Ronnie said, his voice filled with understanding. "We'll be here when you get back."

As Sam stepped out of the comforting embrace of his family home, the midday Georgia heat greeted him like an old friend. The sun beat down relentlessly from a cloudless sky, and the humidity was thick. Each breath felt like a tangible weight on his chest.

Sam squinted against the bright sunlight, his skin tingling as the heat enveloped him like a suffocating blanket. Beads of sweat formed on his brow, trickling down his temples in rivulets as he ventured out into the sweltering afternoon.

Despite the oppressive heat, there was a sense of freedom in the air—a freedom that came with the promise of open skies and endless possibilities. Sam took a deep breath, the warm air filling his lungs as he set out on his walk, his footsteps echoing against the quiet streets.

As he wandered through the familiar neighborhood, the sights and sounds of small-town life surrounded him. The distant hum of lawnmowers, the laughter of children playing in the nearby park, and the rustling of leaves in the gentle breeze reminded him of the simplicity and beauty of everyday life in Pineworth.

As Sam strolled into Pineworth's town square, the sights, sounds, smells, textures, and tastes of the bustling small town enveloped him in a sensory symphony.

The quaint town square stretched before him, framed by historic buildings with weathered facades that told tales of years gone by. Wooden storefronts lined the cobblestone streets, their colorful signs advertising goods and services in bold, hand-painted letters. Vibrant flowers spilled from hanging baskets, adding splashes of color to the sun-drenched scene. People bustled about, their movements creating a lively dance against the backdrop of the picturesque square.

The air was alive with the sounds of small-town life—the cheerful chatter of neighbors catching up on the latest gossip, the rhythmic clatter of horse-drawn carriages making their way through the streets, the jaunty tunes of street musicians serenading passersby with lively melodies. Children's laughter echoed off the walls of nearby buildings, mingling with the distant hum of conversation and the occasional honk of a car horn.

The tantalizing aroma of freshly baked bread wafted from the local bakery, mingling with the rich scent of brewing coffee from the nearby café. The earthy fragrance of pine trees mingled with the sweet perfume of blooming flowers, creating a heady bouquet that hung like a comforting embrace. The savory scent of grilled meats drifted from the barbecue joint on the corner, tempting passersby with promises of mouthwatering delights.

As Sam walked through the town square, the rough texture of the cobblestone streets beneath his feet provided a reassuring solidity, grounding him in the present moment. The warm sunlight kissed his skin, its gentle touch offering a welcome respite from the cool shade of the surrounding buildings. The soft fabric of his shirt clung to his skin in the oppressive heat, a reminder of the relentless Georgia sun beating down from above.

Sam couldn't resist the temptation to sample some fresh produce on display as he passed by the local market. He plucked a ripe peach from a nearby basket and bit into its juicy flesh, the sweet nectar exploding on his tongue in a burst of flavor. The taste of summer lingered on his lips as he continued on his journey through the sensory wonderland of Pineworth's town square.

At that moment, as he immersed himself in his beloved hometown's sights, sounds, smells, textures, and tastes, Sam felt a profound sense of gratitude wash over him. Pineworth may have been a small town in the heart of Georgia, but to him, it was filled with endless beauty, charm, and possibility—a place he was proud to call home.

As Sam settled onto the weathered bench outside the local ice cream shop, he couldn't help but feel a pang of nostalgia wash over him. The familiar sight of the nearby cemetery, where his family lay at rest, reminded him of the generations before him—their wisdom, strength, and legacy.

As he gazed toward the cemetery, his thoughts turned to his grandfather, a man he had admired and respected since childhood. His grandfather had always been a beacon of wisdom and guidance, a source of inspiration in times of uncertainty. He wondered what his grandfather would think of the new times, of the changes sweeping through Pineworth and the world beyond.

His grandfather was a visionary who dared to think outside the box and challenge the status quo. He instilled in Sam a sense of curiosity and a thirst for knowledge, encouraging him to question the world around him and stand up for his beliefs.

But Sam wondered if his grandfather would approve of his stance on the current issues. Would he understand the complexities of the world Sam now found himself navigating? Would he see the same injustices Sam saw, or would his perspective be different?

Sam felt uncertainty gnawing at his insides as he pondered these questions. He longed for his grandfather's wisdom, guidance, and reassurance. But deep down, he knew that his grandfather's spirit lived on within him, guiding him from beyond the grave and urging him to stay true to himself and his values.

With a heavy heart, Sam turned his gaze back toward the bustling town square, freshly churned ice cream wafting through the air.

AS SAM WALKED OUTSIDE the ice cream shop, lost in thought, he noticed his best friend and fellow police officer, Jordan, making his way through the bustling town square. A warm smile spread across Sam's face as he waved in Jordan's direction.

"Hey, Jordan!" Sam called out, his voice carrying across the square.

Jordan turned at the sound of his name, a grin lighting up as he spotted Sam. "Hey, Sam!" he replied, joining him.

As Jordan stood beside him, he couldn't help but notice Sam's thoughtful expression. "What are you up to, buddy?" he asked, his voice filled with genuine curiosity.

Sam sighed, his gaze drifting back toward the cemetery in the distance. "I'm just trying to enjoy my day off," he admitted, his tone tinged with melancholy. I've got to recharge the batteries before I come back in tomorrow."

Jordan understood, placing a comforting hand on Sam's shoulder. "I hear you, man," he said, his voice soft and empathic. "It's been a rough few days for all of us."

Sam offered Jordan a grateful smile, appreciating the understanding in his friend's eyes. "Yeah, it has," he agreed, feeling a sense of camaraderie wash over him. "But we'll get through it together like we always do."

Jordan was more than just a friend to Sam; he was a constant presence in his life, a brother-in-arms who had been by his side since they were kids. Growing up in Pineworth, they shared countless adventures, their bond forged through a shared love of mischief and a mutual desire to make a difference in their community.

When they first met in grade school, Sam and Jordan knew they were destined for something greater. They had dreamed of becoming police officers, upholding the law, and protecting those who couldn't defend themselves. As they grew older, their dreams grew stronger, fueled by a sense of purpose and determination that burned bright within them both.

When they finally joined the police force together, it felt like realizing a lifelong dream. Jordan proved himself to be an exceptional cop with a sharp mind and a strong sense of justice. He was respected by his colleagues and admired by the community, a shining example of what it meant to serve and protect.

But more than that, Jordan was a loyal friend—a steady presence in Sam's life, always there to offer support and guidance when he needed it most. They had each other's backs, through thick and thin, and Sam knew that if he ever found himself in a bind, it would be Jordan he would call for help.

Their friendship was built on trust and mutual respect, a bond that had stood the test of time. As they sat together on the bench in the town square, sharing stories and laughter, Sam couldn't help but feel grateful for the unwavering friendship of his closest confidant—a friendship that had shaped him into the man he is today.

As Jordan and Sam caught up outside the ice cream shop, a concerned citizen approached Jordan, their eyes wide with urgency. "Officer Jordan, I need your help," they said, their voice trembling with anxiety.

Jordan turned his attention to the citizen, his instincts kicking into gear as he listened attentively to their plea. "What's the problem?" he asked, his tone calm and reassuring.

Sam glanced over at Jordan, his friend's professionalism shining through in how he effortlessly handled the situation. He felt a swell of pride in his chest, knowing that Jordan was always ready to lend a helping hand to those in need.

With a nod to Jordan, Sam rose from the bench, offering a wave to his friend as he began to make his way back toward his home. "Take care, Jordan," he called out, his voice carrying across the square. "I'll catch you later."

As he walked away, Sam couldn't help but feel a sense of gratitude for his friend's unwavering dedication to serving their community. He knew that if he ever found himself in a bind, it would

be Jordan; he would call for help. With that comforting thought in mind, Sam continued, grateful for the bond of friendship that had carried him through thick and thin since their school days.

The quiet streets were alive, with children playing and neighbors calling out to one another as they wrapped up their day.

As he passed by the driveways of the quaint homes lining the street, Sam couldn't help but admire the collection of cars parked in them. The vehicles, with their sleek designs and vibrant colors, astonished him.

Among the lineup were cars like the Chevrolet Impala, Ford Mustang, and Dodge Charger. Their boxy shapes and chrome accents exuded an air of retro charm. The sun glinted off their glossy paint jobs, highlighting the distinctive curves and angles that made them stand out on the road.

Amidst the backdrop of automobiles, mothers called out to their children, their voices carrying on the warm evening breeze. "Dinner's ready, kids! Time to come inside!" they called, their words mingling with the laughter of playing children and the distant bark of a dog.

As Sam continued on his way, the sights and sounds of his neighborhood wrapped around him like a comforting blanket, reminding him of the simple joys of suburban life. With each step, he felt a sense of peace wash over him, grateful for the familiar sights and sounds that greeted him on his journey home.

As the sun dipped below the horizon, casting long shadows across the quiet streets, Sam knew that he was exactly where he was meant to be, surrounded by the warmth and love of his community.

Chapter 2
Winds Of Change

The enticing aroma of freshly cooked pancakes wafted through the air, gently nudging Sam awake from his slumber. As he slowly opened his eyes, the comforting scent enveloped him, coaxing a sleepy smile to his lips. Pancakes could only mean one thing: it was time to rise and shine for another day on the beat.

Rolling out of bed, Sam stretched his limbs, relishing the sensation of waking up to the delicious scent of breakfast. With renewed energy, he quickly dressed in his crisp uniform, anticipating the day ahead, replacing the lingering traces of sleepiness.

Heading to the kitchen, Sam found his mother, Eleanor, standing over the stove, expertly flipping pancakes with practiced ease. The sizzle of batter hitting the hot griddle filled the room, punctuated by the occasional soft hiss as each pancake cooked to golden perfection.

"Morning, Mom," Sam greeted her with a warm smile, the enticing aroma of breakfast filling his senses.

"Good morning, Sam," Eleanor replied, returning his smile as she deftly flipped another pancake. "I figured you could use a hearty breakfast before heading out."

Sam's stomach rumbled in agreement, the irresistible scent of pancakes making his mouth water. "Thanks, Mom," he said gratefully, sitting at the kitchen table.

As Eleanor plated up a generous stack of pancakes, Sam couldn't help but feel a swell of gratitude for his mother's thoughtfulness. Breakfast may have been a simple gesture, but it was a reminder of the love and care that surrounded him, even in the midst of his demanding job.

With each bite of fluffy pancake and drizzle of maple syrup, Sam felt his energy levels soar, readying him for the day ahead. As he finished his meal, he bid his mother farewell with a kiss on the cheek, a renewed sense of purpose propelling him forward.

Sam approached his wardrobe with purpose as he prepared for another day on the beat. From a young age, he had dreamed of wearing the uniform of the Pineworth Police Department, and now, after four years on the force, it had become a familiar part of his daily routine.

Sam pulled on his crisp blue shirt with practiced ease, smooth fabric against his skin as he rapidly fastened the buttons. Each piece of his uniform held a significance—a symbol of his dedication to serving and protecting the community he had grown up in.

Next came the neatly pressed and creased navy trousers, a testament to Sam's attention to detail. As he slipped them on, he couldn't help but feel a swell of pride at how far he had come since joining the force. From a wide-eyed rookie to a seasoned officer, he had weathered the challenges and triumphs of life on the beat with determination and grit.

Finally, Sam reached for his badge, the gleaming metal emblem a tangible reminder of his oath to uphold the law and safeguard the lives of those around him. As he pinned it to his chest, he felt a sense of purpose wash over him, his resolve strengthened by the weight of responsibility that came with wearing the badge.

With his uniform complete, Sam took a moment to glance in the mirror, the reflection staring back at him as a testament to the dreams he had pursued since childhood. From the moment he had first donned the uniform, he had known that this was where he belonged—out on the streets, making a difference in the lives of others.

As he made his way out the door, ready to face whatever challenges the day may bring, Sam couldn't help but smile at the thought of the little boy who had once dreamed of wearing the badge. He may have grown up since then, but his passion for serving his community burned as brightly as ever, guiding him forward with unwavering determination.

As Sam stepped out into the morning sunlight, the weight of responsibility settled heavily on his shoulders. At 24 years old, he couldn't help but wonder why he was still living at home while most of his peers were out on their own, building their own lives. But as he glanced back at the familiar walls of his family home, the reason became painfully clear.

His father's health had been in decline for years now, a fact that weighed heavily on Sam's heart. The once strong and vibrant man he had looked up to as a child was now frail and needed constant care. Sam knew his mother couldn't handle it alone, and he couldn't bear the thought of leaving her to shoulder the burden alone.

With each passing day, Sam's sense of duty to his family grew stronger, outweighing any desire he may have had for independence. His father needed him, and he would do whatever it took to ensure that his parents were cared for, even if it meant putting his dreams on hold.

As Sam stepped into his car, a 1971 AMC Matador, a sense of pride washed over him. The Matador's distinctive body, with its angular front end and streamlined profile, stood out amidst the sea of modern cars lining the streets.

Sliding into the driver's seat, Sam took a moment to admire the car's interior. The dashboard, adorned with wood paneling and chrome accents, exuded elegance. The vinyl seats offered a comfortable embrace as Sam settled in for the day ahead.

As he turned the key in the ignition, the engine roared to life with a satisfying rumble, echoing through the cabin like a symphony of power and precision. The scent of leather and gasoline filled the air, a familiar fragrance that spoke of countless journeys and adventures yet to come.

Sam had already grown fond of the car, though he had only been assigned the Matador a week ago. Its reliable performance and muscle style made it a joy to drive, and it is a faithful companion on the streets of Pineworth. As he pulled out of the driveway and onto the road, a smile spread across his face, the thrill of the open road beckoning him forward.

With the windows rolled down and the wind in his hair, Sam felt a sense of freedom wash over him, the Matador carrying him toward whatever challenges the day may bring. It may have been just a car to some, but to Sam, it symbolized his passion for the job—a reminder that even in the midst of change, some things would always remain the same.

As Sam parked his vehicle in the station lot, he spotted Jordan leaning against the entrance, a severe expression etched on his face. Stepping out of the car, Sam approached his friend, exchanging a nod of greeting.

"Morning, Jordan," Sam greeted, noting the tension in his friend's posture. "What's on your mind?"

Jordan glanced around before leaning in closer, his voice low with concern. "Sam, tensions are high right now," he murmured, eyes scanning the area for eavesdroppers. "Racial tensions, to be exact."

Sam's heart sank at the mention of racial tensions. It wasn't a secret that the winds of change were sweeping through Pineworth, bringing a wave of uncertainty and unrest. But to hear Jordan confirm it only solidified the gravity of the situation.

"What's going on?" Sam asked, his voice tinged with apprehension.

Jordan sighed, running a hand through his hair in frustration. "City Hall's planning a meeting to discuss the desegregation of schools," he explained, his tone heavy with significance. "They expect things to get heated, so they want us all there for security."

Sam's stomach churned at the thought of the volatile situation that awaited them. Desegregation was a necessary step toward equality, but it was also a deeply contentious issue that could further divide the community.

"Great," Sam muttered, a sense of foreboding settling over him like a dark cloud. "Another day in paradise."

Jordan offered him a sympathetic smile, clapping a hand on his shoulder in a gesture of solidarity. "Hang in there, buddy," he said, his voice filled with determination. "We'll get through this together."

As Sam and Jordan stepped into the station, they were greeted by the familiar sight of their colleagues bustling about, preparing for the day ahead. Making their way to the briefing room, they found Chief Johnson waiting for them at the front, his expression grave as he addressed the assembled officers.

"Morning, everyone," Chief Johnson greeted, his voice commanding attention as he surveyed the room. "As you all know, tensions are running high in our city right now, especially with the upcoming meeting at City Hall."

The room fell silent, the weight of Chief Johnson's words hanging heavy in the air. Sam and Jordan exchanged a knowing glance, their apprehension mirrored in each other's eyes.

"Our goal today is simple," Chief Johnson continued, his tone firm. "We're here to maintain order and prevent violence. We're not here to take sides or escalate tensions any further."

He paused, his gaze sweeping across the room as he emphasized his next point. "I can't stress this enough, folks. All eyes are on us today. We don't want to see any of you on the news tonight for the wrong reasons."

Sam felt a knot form in his stomach at the reminder of the scrutiny they would be under. The last thing he wanted was to become a headline, especially in a volatile situation.

Chief Johnson's words served as a sobering reminder of the gravity of their duty as law enforcement officers. In a time of uncertainty and unrest, they were tasked with keeping the peace and upholding the law, no matter the challenges they faced.

As Chief Johnson concluded his briefing, he delivered one final message that sent a ripple of anticipation through the room.

"Oh, and one more thing," he announced, his voice carrying a note of gravity. "Mayor Carter will be in attendance at today's meeting."

The mention of Mayor Carter, a figure of authority and influence in both the community and the police department, sparked a renewed sense of focus among the officers. Sam felt a surge of determination wash over him at the thought of being in the presence of such a respected figure.

"Let's make sure we're all in tip-top shape," Chief Johnson continued, his tone leaving no room for doubt. "We need to show Mayor Carter that we're capable of handling this situation with professionalism and grace."

Sam exchanged a glance with Jordan, both of them silently acknowledging the weight of Chief Johnson's words. The presence of Mayor Carter elevated the importance of their mission, adding an extra layer of pressure to an already tense situation.

As Sam stepped out of the briefing room, he exchanged a nod with Jordan, the weight of their upcoming assignment lingering in the air between them. But despite the gravity of their duty, Sam couldn't help but feel a sense of pride in the way policing had evolved in recent years.

From his perspective, policing at this time had seen a notable rise in community involvement—a shift toward a more proactive, collaborative approach to law enforcement. Gone were the days of simply reacting to crime after it occurred; instead, officers like Sam were encouraged to engage with their community on a deeper level, forging bonds of trust and understanding that went beyond mere enforcement.

Sam found himself drawn to this new model of policing, one that emphasized partnership and cooperation over authoritarianism and division. He enjoyed the opportunity to interact with the people he served, to listen to their concerns, and to work together to find solutions to the challenges facing their community.

Whether it was organizing neighborhood watch programs, hosting community events, or simply walking the beat and chatting with residents, Sam relished every opportunity to connect with the people he was sworn to protect. He believed that by building solid relationships with the community, they could not only prevent crime but also foster a sense of unity and resilience that would withstand whatever challenges came their way.

As he made his way out of the station, Sam couldn't help but feel a sense of optimism for the future of policing in Pineworth. With each passing day, he was reminded that the true strength of law enforcement lay not in the weapons they carried or the authority they wielded but in the trust and cooperation of the people they served.

As Sam strolled through the familiar streets of the town square, his eyes caught sight of a newspaper stand nestled among the bustling shops and cafes. Curiosity piqued, he approached the stand, his gaze drawn to the bold headline splashed across the front page:

"Governor CARTER STUNS WITH INAUGURATION SPEECH"

The words leaped out at Sam, commanding his attention in an instant. Governor Carter's inauguration had been the talk of the town, but Sam hadn't had a chance to catch the full speech yet. With a sense of intrigue, he reached out and grabbed a copy of the newspaper, eager to delve into the details.

As he skimmed the article, Sam found himself captivated by the governor's words, his vision for the future of the nation laid out with clarity and conviction. The mention of ending segregation struck a chord with Sam, reminding him of the challenges facing his own community in Pineworth.

Governor Carter's bold stance on civil rights sent ripples of hope through Sam's heart, a reminder that change was possible, even in the face of adversity. As a police officer, he knew that the road ahead would be difficult, but the governor's words served as a beacon of inspiration, urging him to continue fighting for justice and equality in his own corner of the world.

As Sam continued his walk through the town square, a palpable tension hung in the air, almost tangible in its intensity. He couldn't shake the feeling that something was amiss, a sense of unease prickling at the back of his neck.

As he passed by a group of elderly white men gathered on a bench, their hushed voices caught his attention. Sam slowed his pace, pretending to admire a nearby storefront as he strained to listen to their conversation.

"I can't believe they're even considering integrating the schools," one of the men muttered, his voice heavy with disapproval. "It's just not right."

His companion shouted in agreement, his expression sour. "We've always had our own schools here in Pineworth," he added, his tone laced with resentment. "Why should we have to change now?"

Sam felt a knot form in his stomach at the man's words, their attitudes a stark reminder of the deep-seated prejudices that still lingered within the community.

As the minutes ticked by, the town square began to fill with people, their presence lending an air of anticipation to the gathering. Sam watched from a distance as more and more individuals streamed into the square, their faces etched with determination and purpose.

Some carried signs bearing messages of support for desegregation, their bold letters proclaiming slogans of equality and justice. Others arrived in groups, their voices raised in spirited conversation as they discussed the importance of the upcoming meeting at the town hall.

But amid the sea of faces, Sam couldn't help but notice a palpable tension that hung in the air, a sense of division that threatened to fracture the unity of the community. He knew that the issue of desegregation was a deeply contentious one, with passionate voices on both sides of the debate.

As he watched the crowd continue to swell, Sam felt a renewed sense of responsibility settles over him. Today's meeting would be a pivotal moment for Pineworth, a chance to confront the challenges of the past and embrace a future of inclusivity and progress.

As the minutes ticked by, the town square began to fill with people, their presence lending an air of anticipation to the gathering. Sam watched from a distance as more and more individuals streamed into the square, their faces etched with determination and purpose.

Some carried signs bearing messages of support for desegregation, their bold letters proclaiming slogans of equality and justice. Others arrived in groups, their voices raised in spirited conversation as they discussed the importance of the upcoming meeting at the town hall.

But amid the sea of faces, Sam couldn't help but notice a palpable tension that hung in the air, a sense of division that threatened to fracture the unity of the community. He knew that the issue of desegregation was a deeply contentious one, with passionate voices on both sides of the debate.

As he watched the crowd continue to swell, Sam felt a renewed sense of responsibility settles over him. Today's meeting would be a pivotal moment for Pineworth, a chance to confront the challenges of the past and embrace a future of inclusivity and progress.

As Mayor Carter arrived at the town hall, a ripple of surprise spread through the crowd. But what truly caught everyone off guard was the presence of his young son, Seth, by his side. The sight of the mayor accompanied by his child sent a powerful message—a reminder that this meeting was not just for adults but for all ages.

Sam watched as Mayor Carter and Seth made their way through the crowd, their presence drawing curious glances and whispers of admiration. It was clear that the mayor's decision to bring his son was a deliberate one, a move to underscore the importance of a peaceful and inclusive dialogue.

As they entered the town hall, Sam felt a swell of hope wash over him. The presence of Seth served as a tangible reminder of the future they were fighting for—a future where all children, regardless of race or background, could grow up in a community free from fear and discrimination.

With Mayor Carter's gesture serving as a catalyst, Sam felt a renewed sense of determination settles over the crowd. It was a reminder that they were all in this together, united in their quest for justice and equality.

As the city council announced the plan to integrate the public schools, the news was met with a mixed reaction from the crowd. While some silently sat in agreement, others erupted in a chorus of boos, their discontent palpable in the air.

Amongst the sea of faces, Sam's attention was drawn to a young woman standing near the back of the crowd. Though he couldn't quite place where he had seen her before, there was something familiar about her demeanor—a quiet strength that radiated from her as she stood resolute amidst the turmoil.

While the boos echoed around her, the young mother remained undeterred, her hands clapping in applause at the announcement. It was a bold gesture, one that stood in stark contrast to the hostility of those around her.

Sam couldn't help but admire her courage in the face of adversity. In that moment, she embodied the spirit of resilience and determination that he had come to admire in the people of Pineworth. She was a reminder that even in the darkest of times, there were still those who dared to stand up for what was right, regardless of the consequences.

As the city council announced the lineup of speakers, the first to take the stage was Ted Phillips, a respected figure from one of Pineworth's founding families. His presence commanded attention, a reminder of the deep-rooted history and influence that his family held in the community.

Ted began by thanking Mayor Daniel Carter for organizing the event, his words dripping with politeness and formality. But as he delved into his reasons for opposing school integration, the tone of his speech grew more pointed, his arguments laced with concern and skepticism.

Citing the potential for discord and unrest among students, Ted expressed doubts about the feasibility of integration, questioning whether children from different backgrounds would be able to "mesh" together harmoniously. His words struck a chord with some members of the crowd, eliciting nods of agreement and murmurs of approval.

But it was his next question that caused a ripple of unease to spread through the audience. "What next?" he asked, his voice tinged with apprehension. "Will we need to station police officers in our schools to ensure safety?"

Sam felt a surge of frustration rises within him at Ted's insinuation. It was a thinly veiled threat, a suggestion that integration would inevitably lead to violence and chaos.

As the next speaker was called to the podium, Sam's attention sharpened, and to his surprise, it was the young woman he had noticed earlier—the one who had bravely applauded amidst the boos. Anida Woodward, her name resonating with familiarity as the crowd erupted into applause, a testament to her standing within the community.

Sam watched with a sense of intrigue as Anida approached the podium, her presence commanding attention despite her youthful appearance. There was a quiet confidence about her, a sense of determination that belied her age as she prepared to address the crowd.

As Anida began to speak, her voice clear and steady, Sam found himself captivated by her words.

"Ladies and gentlemen," she began, "Thank you for the opportunity to address you today. My name is Anida Woodward, and I stand before you not just as a member of this community but as a mother—a mother who wants nothing more than to see her daughter grow up in a world where she is treated with dignity and respect, where her opportunities are not limited by the color of her skin.

As I look around this room, I see the faces of my neighbors, my friends, my fellow citizens. And I can't help but wonder: Are we truly living up to the ideals of freedom and equality that our nation was founded upon? Are we providing every child in this community with the same chance to succeed?

I stand here today as a voice for my daughter and for all the children who have been denied the opportunities they deserve simply because of the color of their skin. My daughter is bright, talented, and full of potential. But every day, she goes to a school where the resources are scarce, the teachers are overworked, and the opportunities are limited.

I refuse to accept that this is the best we can do for our children. I refuse to accept that my daughter and others like her should be held back by a system that is stacked against them from the start.

My family has a long history of service to this country. My ancestors fought in wars, they shed their blood, and they made sacrifices so that future generations could enjoy the freedoms that they fought so hard to protect. And yet, here we are, still fighting for those same freedoms, still struggling to ensure that every child has access to a quality education, regardless of their race or background.

But I believe that we can do better. I think that we have a moral obligation to do better—for the sake of our children, for the sake of our community, for the sake of our future.

So, let us come together; let us stand united in our commitment to justice and equality. Let us not be content to simply accept the status quo, but let us strive to build a better world for our children—one where every child has the chance to thrive, to succeed, and to fulfill their dreams.

Thank you."

She spoke not just with passion but with a depth of understanding that seemed to transcend her years, her eloquence drawing the audience in as she articulated her vision for a more inclusive and equitable future.

With each word she spoke, Anida challenged the status quo, calling on her fellow citizens to embrace change and work together to build a better tomorrow. She spoke of the importance of diversity and representation in the classroom, of the need to confront the injustices of the past and forge a path toward reconciliation and healing.

As Sam listened to her impassioned plea, he couldn't help but feel a swell of admiration for Anida. Here was a young woman who dared to speak truth to power, who refused to be silenced in the face of adversity. She was a reminder that courage knew no bounds and that the voices of the marginalized and oppressed would not be ignored.

As Anida concluded her speech to thunderous applause, Sam felt a surge of hope wash over him. In her words, he saw the promise of a brighter future—a future where all children, regardless of race or background, could learn and grow together in a community that celebrated their differences rather than feared them.

As the council members finally announced their decision to integrate Pineworth High School, the reaction from the crowd was immediate and visceral. Cheers of approval mingled with boos of dissent, creating a cacophony of conflicting emotions that filled the air.

Amidst the chaos, small outbreaks of confrontations began to erupt within the crowd, tensions running high as emotions threatened to boil over. Sam felt a knot form in his stomach as he surveyed the scene, knowing that it was up to him and his fellow officers to restore order and prevent the situation from spiraling out of control.

Chief Johnson's gaze met Sam's, and in that silent exchange, Sam understood the gravity of the situation. It was clear that they needed to act swiftly and decisively to quell the unrest and ensure the safety of everyone present.

With a sense of determination, Sam sprang into action, moving swiftly through the crowd to intervene in the confrontations that had broken out. He called out commands, his voice firm and authoritative as he urged people to step back and calm down.

Around him, his fellow officers followed suit, working together to diffuse the tension and restore order to the chaotic scene. It was a delicate balancing act, but they knew that the stakes were too high to allow the situation to escalate any further.

Slowly but surely, the crowd began to quiet down, the intensity of their emotions gradually subsiding as order was restored. Sam felt a sense of relief wash over him as he surveyed the scene, grateful that they had been able to avert a potential disaster.

As the meeting resumed and the council members continued their deliberations, Sam remained vigilant, his eyes scanning the crowd for any signs of further trouble. It was a reminder of the challenges they faced in their quest for equality and justice, but also a testament to the resilience and determination of those who refused to be silenced in the face of adversity.

With Chief Johnson's silent nod of approval, Sam knew that they had done their job well. And as they stood guard, ready to uphold the peace and protect the rights of all who had gathered before them, he felt a renewed sense of pride in the work that they did, knowing that they were making a difference, one small step at a time.

As the meeting drew to a close, the tension that had filled the air began to dissipate, replaced by a sense of weary resignation. Slowly but surely, the crowd started to disperse, the once bustling town hall now emptying out as people headed their separate ways.

Sam watched as the attendees filed out of the building, their faces reflecting a myriad of emotions—some still simmering with anger, others wearied by the intensity of the discussions that had taken place. It had been a long and tumultuous evening, one that had tested the resolve of everyone present.

As he stood guard at the entrance, Sam couldn't help but feel a sense of relief that the meeting had ended without any major incidents. It had been touch and go there for a while, but somehow, they had managed to keep the peace and prevent the situation from spiraling out of control.

As the last of the attendees made their way out into the night, Sam allowed himself a moment of quiet reflection. Despite the challenges they had faced, he felt a glimmer of hope for the future—a hope that perhaps, one day, they could overcome the divisions that had long plagued their community and build a better, more inclusive society for all.

With a sigh, Sam turned to join his fellow officers, ready to debrief and discuss the events of the evening.

As Sam stood among his fellow officers, discussing the events of the evening, his attention was momentarily drawn away by the sight of the young woman leaving the building. He couldn't help but admire her courage and eloquence during her speech, and a part of him wanted to approach her and offer a word of appreciation.

But as he hesitated, a sense of duty washed over him. In uniform, he was bound by a code of impartiality—a commitment to upholding the law and serving the community without bias or favoritism. Approaching the young woman in such a manner could be perceived as a breach of that code, and Sam knew that he had to maintain his professionalism, even in moments of personal admiration.

With a sigh, Sam watched silently as the young woman disappeared into the night, her figure receding into the darkness. He hoped that she knew the impact of her words, the way they had resonated with so many in the crowd.

Chapter 3
Air Thickening Tension

AS THE DAYS PASSED in Pineworth, the atmosphere seemed to crackle with tension, the aftermath of the town hall meeting lingering like a storm cloud over the community. In the wake of the decision to integrate Pineworth High School, emotions ran high, and divisions within the town deepened.

For Sam and his fellow officers, the streets of Pineworth felt like a powder keg ready to explode at any moment. They patrolled the town with a sense of vigilance, their eyes scanning the crowds for any signs of unrest or dissent. But beneath the facade of calm, they could sense the undercurrent of unease, a feeling that something was brewing beneath the surface.

As he made his rounds through the town, Sam couldn't shake the feeling of foreboding that hung in the air. He knew that tensions were running high on both sides of the debate, and he feared that it wouldn't take much to ignite the simmering resentment and anger that lurked just beneath the surface.

As Sam patrolled the streets of Pineworth, his radio crackled to life with a call from dispatch.

"Unit 23, we have a report of a suspicious person in progress on Maple Street," the dispatcher's voice came through loud and clear.

Sam's grip tightened on the steering wheel as he acknowledged the call. "Copy that, dispatch. I'm en route to Maple Street now," he responded, his voice steady despite the urgency of the situation.

"10-4, Unit 23. The suspect is reported to be a young individual acting suspiciously in the yards of the neighborhood. Approach with caution," the dispatcher warned, her tone serious.

"Copy that, dispatch. I'll proceed with caution," Sam replied, his senses on high alert as he navigated the streets toward Maple Street.

As he turned onto Maple Street, Sam scanned the area for any signs of trouble. The neighborhood was quiet, the houses bathed in the soft glow of streetlights. But as he rounded a corner, his headlights illuminated a figure darting between the yards.

Sam brought his patrol car to a halt, activating the siren to catch the attention of the young boy who had come to a stop in a nearby yard. As the boy turned to face him, Sam could see the worry etched on his young face.

Rolling down his window, Sam called out to the boy, his voice firm but gentle. "Hey there, everything okay?" he asked, his gaze assessing the situation.

The boy, no older than thirteen, hesitated for a moment before responding. "Yeah, I'm okay. Just out here looking for my dog," he explained, his voice tinged with a hint of nervousness.

Sam studied the boy carefully, noting the sincerity in his eyes. Despite his initial suspicions, there was something about the boy's demeanor that rang true.

"Your dog, huh? What's his name?" Sam inquired, keeping his tone calm and reassuring.

The boy shifted nervously on his feet before answering. "His name's Max. He got out of the yard, and I've been looking for him all over," he explained, his voice tinged with worry.

Sam considered the boy's words for a moment, weighing his options. Despite the relatively late hour and the unusual circumstances, there was no reason to doubt the boy's story.

Sam turned his attention to the middle-aged man who had emerged from the nearby house, his voice filled with anger and suspicion. As the man approached, Sam could see the tension in his body language, his eyes fixed firmly on the young boy standing nearby.

"Hey, calm down," Sam called out, stepping out of his patrol car to intervene. "I understand your concern, but let's not jump to conclusions here."

The man's face contorted with frustration as he glared at Sam. "He has no business being here. I called it in because I saw him lurking around my yard. Who knows what he's up to," he insisted, his voice trembling with anger.

Sam held up a hand in a gesture of peace, trying to defuse the situation before it escalated any further. "I hear you, but the boy says he's just looking for his lost dog. Let's give him the benefit of the doubt for now," he suggested, hoping to ease the man's concerns.

BUT THE MAN HAD NONE of it, and his distrust was apparent in every word he spoke. "I don't care what he says. This is my property, and I won't have strangers snooping around here," he declared, his tone growing more confrontational by the moment.

Sam exchanged a frustrated glance with the boy, knowing that the situation was quickly spiraling out of control. With tensions running high, he knew that he needed to act quickly to defuse the situation before it turned ugly.

"Look, I understand you're upset, but let's handle this calmly," Sam urged, his voice firm but measured. "I'll talk to the boy, make sure he's on his way. And if you have any more concerns, you can call us, alright?"

The man grumbled under his breath but begrudgingly agreed to leave it to Sam. As Sam turned back to the boy, he could feel the weight of the situation bearing down on him. With a silent prayer for peace, he approached the young boy once more, determined to resolve the problem as peacefully as possible.

"Hey, I think it's time for you to go. How about this? I'll keep an eye out for Max, too. But for now, you should head home. It's late," Sam said, offering the boy a reassuring smile.

The boy walked away, his shoulders hunched with disappointment, and Sam turned his attention back to the middle-aged man who had made the revolting comment. The man's words hung in the air like a toxic cloud, poisoning the atmosphere with their bigotry.

"You bring them into the school. Next, they're in your neighborhood," the man sneered, his tone dripping with disdain.

Sam felt a surge of anger and disbelief at the man's callousness.

After leaving the man, Sam now had time alone to process his feelings towards him. It wasn't that he disliked the man. He disliked the way the situation was handled. Was the kid wrong to be on his property? Sure.

And maybe that was it. Perhaps it isn't that race was an issue or wasn't. It is whether or not a situation is handled correctly that determines if the element of race, or any other element for that matter, plays a part.

While cruising along, he spots his buddy Jordan watching vehicles on the side of the road. He decides to accompany him.

"What's up, man?" He says to him.

Jordan responds, "Oh, you know, looking for trouble before it finds me."

"I hear ya. Let me ask you a question?"

"Shoot," Jordan replies.

"I just got off that call with that little kid. The owner of the house made a comment about the schools, and it just irked me. That situation ever happened to you?"

Jordan took off his sunglasses, looked at Sam, and responded. "Plenty man. We aren't always going to deal with people who agree with us or have the same views. You did the right thing there calming down the situation. Idk why people around here are so freaked out. It's not like we are the first city to integrate. We are actually one of the last."

Sam smiled at his remark and added, "Yeah, it just feels like the city has been surpassed in so many ways in terms of community. And not just on race. I mean, imagine another town that will have the same last name as mayor forever like this."

"Yeah, man, it is like that here. But it's also what makes our town unique. We know who we are. We are a town run by a few rich families. As long as those families don't run us to the ground, I'll stay in my lane." Jordan answered back.

Sam understood where Jordan was coming from. He was well aware of the history of the town. How the "founding families" were always around and in control. He also knew that although this was something that irked him, he saw how most people could overlook it. The problems they now face were far and away more important to people.

As the workday wore on, Sam found his way into the cemetery. He would often patrol inside the cemetery. It was a way for him to still do his job and also get peace and quiet.

While walking along, reading the names on the rows of stones, Sam spotted two women walking in his direction. As they got closer he could make out that one of them was Anida Woodward. He thought about just letting her pass by him. In the end, he knew he had to say something, or he would regret it.

"Good afternoon," he greeted them warmly, extending a hand in greeting. "I'm Officer Sam Anderson. I don't believe we've had the pleasure of meeting."

The young woman's eyes widened in recognition, a hint of surprise crossing her features. "Oh, hello, Officer Anderson," she replied, her voice warm and welcoming. "I'm Anida, and this is my sister, Natalie. It's nice to meet you."

Beside her, Natalie offered a polite nod of acknowledgment, her gaze meeting Sam's for a moment before darting away. There was a shy reserve to her demeanor, a sense of quiet curiosity that Sam found endearing.

As Sam exchanged pleasantries with Anida and her sister Natalie, he couldn't help but steal a glance at the latter. She stood beside her sister, her posture straight and poised, her features exuding a quiet elegance that caught Sam's attention.

She appeared to be around his age, with soft, chestnut-colored hair cascading in gentle waves around her shoulders. Her almond-shaped eyes, a warm shade of hazel, held a hint of mystery, their depths betraying a quiet reserve that intrigued Sam.

Natalie's beauty was undeniable, her features delicate and refined, yet there was a subtle strength to her presence that drew Sam's gaze. Despite her reserved demeanor, there was an underlying confidence in the way she carried herself, a sense of self-assurance that spoke volumes.

As Sam took in her appearance, he couldn't help but feel a flutter of attraction stir within him. There was something magnetic about Natalie, something that captivated him in a way he couldn't quite explain.

As Sam conversed with the sisters, he couldn't help but feel compelled to express his admiration for Anida's impassioned speech at the town hall meeting. With a genuine smile, he turned to her, his voice sincere.

"Anida, I just wanted to say that your speech at the town hall meeting was truly wonderful and very powerful," Sam remarked, his words carrying a sense of genuine appreciation. "You spoke from the heart, and your words resonated with so many people. It takes courage to stand up for what you believe in, and you did it with grace and conviction."

Anida's eyes sparkled with gratitude, a warm smile spreading across her face. "Thank you, Officer Anderson," she replied, her voice tinged with emotion. "It means a lot to hear that."

Beside her, Natalie offered a supportive nod, her expression reflecting a silent acknowledgment of her sister's bravery. In that moment, amidst the tranquil surroundings of the cemetery, Sam felt a sense of camaraderie with the sisters—a shared understanding of the struggles they faced and a shared hope for a better future.

As their conversation began to wind down, Sam realized it was time for him to wrap up his shift. With a friendly smile, he addressed Anida, feeling a subtle tug of regret at the prospect of parting ways. His gaze briefly flickered to Anida's sister, Natalie, as he spoke.

"It's been great getting to know y'all," Sam said, his tone genuine as he exchanged nods with each of them. "Your company made the day go by faster."

Anida returned his smile graciously, while Natalie offered a shy nod in response. Sam noticed a hint of color in Natalie's cheeks, and though he tried to suppress it, he couldn't ignore the flicker of warmth that stirred within him.

With a final wave, Sam turned to leave, his thoughts lingering on the brief encounter with the sisters. As he made his way back to the station, he couldn't shake the feeling of intrigue that Natalie had sparked within him.

There was something about her quiet demeanor that left him curious, and he found himself looking forward to the possibility of seeing her again. And with that thought in mind, Sam continued on his way, the memory of their meeting lingering in his mind like a gentle breeze.

Chapter 4
A Long Days Rest

THE HEART OF SUMMER had arrived in Pineworth. The sound of grass being cut rang out as Sam sat on the porch of his home. The sound of a metal spoon spinning against the glass as his mom makes her famous fresh lemonade.

"Here's your glass" his mom says as she hands him the cool drink. He takes a sip. The shock of the ice hitting his lips sending a refreshing signal through him.

"Thank you," He replied.

"So, what is in store for you today?" She asks.

"I thought I'd spend the day here with y'all," he said with a smile. He was happy here. Also, knowing that if his dad needed something, it wouldn't just fall to his mom to help.

"Son," she began, "we know you have sacrificed a lot by staying here with us. We also understand that you work very hard. You deserve to spend your day off somewhere with friends or doing something that pleases you. We will be okay here. We live in a small town. If we need you, we can find you, I promise."

Sam appreciated the support from his mom. He had often been so focused on being there for his family that he had put himself and his own life in the rearview.

A warm feeling erupted from him, knowing that his mom was thinking of him as much as he was thinking of her.

"You're right," He told her. "I really do need a day to myself. Thank you for noticing. And thank you for the lemonade. It is as good as ever."

He hugged his mom and went to grab his keys.

A day to himself!

Blocking out all worries and just enjoying the day. It seemed foreign. But that is just what he needed.

He yelled "See y'all later" to his parents and jumped in his old pick up truck. It was an old red and rusty truck. A gift from his uncle when he was eighteen. Working on it had brought him peace when his dad was going through his health issues.

The engine started up with a roar, and the feeling of the vibration surged through him.

Riding down the street he could see kids running around. Some are playing football. Others drinking water from water hoses. One family had huge smiles on their faces as Dad cut open a fresh watermelon.

He drove to the town square and parked at the ice cream shop. While stepping out of his truck, he sees Natalie walking out.

His heart skipped a beat as he took in her radiant smile and the way the sunlight played off her hair, casting a golden glow around her. Her eyes sparkled with warmth and kindness, drawing him in like a magnet.

At that moment, Sam couldn't help but marvel at Natalie's beauty. Her gentle features seemed to hold a world of depth and sincerity, and he found himself captivated by the way she carried herself with grace and confidence. Her laughter floated through the air, filling him with a sense of joy and anticipation.

Sam gets out of his truck and walks towards her.

With each step closer to her, Sam felt a rush of emotions swirling within him – excitement, nervousness, and a profound sense of gratitude for the opportunity to spend time with someone as excellent as Natalie. He couldn't wait to open the door for her and immerse himself in her presence, knowing that every moment with her was a treasure to be cherished.

He ran to hold the door open for her as she walked out.

"Thank you." she says then, as she remembers him out of his uniform, "Officer Anderson?"

"Please call me Sam." He said back. "How are you today?"

"I am good. I am just headed for a walk around town. Don't see why not and waste a great day."

"Agreed. I plan on doing the same," he said back.

"Well, I wouldn't mind some company." She started. "It wouldn't hurt having a police walk with me either."

He smiled and replied, "Sure thing."

They walked along the town square. Each gave the other some knowledge about the buildings they passed by. Sharing childhood experiences.

When they passed by the police station, she said, "Oh look, it's your home away from home."

He responded, "Oh yeah. The last place I want to think about today."

"It can't be all that bad working as a policeman in this town, is it"? She asks.

"Bad isn't the word." He began as they continued their walk past the station.

"I love my job. I love to help people. I think we do way more good for the community than we do bad. I just think that with all the separation in our community, more can be done to support certain people."

She looked at him in astonishment. He wasn't sure if it was what he said or the way he said it.

"What?" he asked.

"Nothing, I am just not sure I have met anyone like you. You care more than anyone. About the struggles of people that aren't your own. I commend you for that."

He thought for a minute and responded "I thank you. But I don't think I should be commended. I think we all make up this town. The great Pineworth, Georgia."

They laughed together at his statement and he continued "No but really, I think we should all be there for each other. We are all tied together. If we have a group of people that are only wanting equal opportunity it seems like a small ask to me."

"I happen to think the same." She said, smiling as she looked ahead.

He noticed the same look she had when they met. The smile that could brighten the road ahead in the pitch black.

He wasn't sure what she wanted out of this friendship or acquaintance. So he was happy just to speak with her.

"You know, they say the whole industry will move out of here in a few years' time. They employ a lot of people in my neighborhood. They are all worried about what will happen if that occurs." She states.

"Yeah, I have heard the same. I just hope those affected can find jobs somewhere." He acknowledged.

As their walk continued, the conversation turned into a more cheerful one. Sam would tell her some of his stories about being on patrol in the city.

She told him about getting her nursing degree.

"I just got it last weekend. I applied to work in the Pineworth ER. I am hoping they accept me there so I don't have to move away from my family to look for a job."

"I hope so too. You are pretty cool to have around." He said back with a smile.

As Sam walked alongside Natalie, he couldn't help but admire her in a more human, relatable way. Her hair, while not perfectly styled, had a natural, tousled look to it that gave her an air of effortless beauty. Stray strands occasionally danced in the breeze, framing her face in a way that made her seem approachable and down-to-earth.

Her eyes held a warmth that drew him in, not just for their color but for the genuine kindness and understanding that shone through them. They sparkled with laughter as she recounted a funny story from her day, and Sam found himself smiling along with her, enjoying the moment of shared camaraderie.

Her smile was infectious, lighting up her face and spreading joy to those around her. It wasn't flawless, but it was genuine, with a hint of mischief that hinted at a playful side to her personality. Sam couldn't help but feel a flutter in his chest every time she flashed that smile in his direction.

As they walked and talked, Sam realized that it wasn't just Natalie's physical appearance that made her beautiful—it was her authenticity, her warmth, and her ability to make him feel at ease in her presence. He felt grateful for the opportunity to spend time with her, to get to know the real person behind the captivating exterior.

At that moment, as they shared stories and laughter, Sam knew that he was drawn to Natalie not just for her beauty but for the genuine connection they shared. And as they continued on their walk, he couldn't help but feel excited about the possibility of what their friendship might blossom into.

As they continued their walk, Natalie glanced at her watch and sighed softly. "I hate to cut our time short, but I really should be heading home soon," she said, a hint of reluctance in her voice.

Sam understood though he couldn't help but feel a twinge of disappointment at the thought of their time together coming to an end. "I completely understand," he replied, offering her a warm smile. "Would you like me to drive you home?"

Natalie hesitated for a moment before nodding, a grateful smile spreading across her face. "That would be lovely, thank you," she said, her voice tinged with appreciation.

Sam felt a surge of happiness at her acceptance, eager for the chance to spend a little more time in her company. With a nod, he gestured for her to follow him as they made their way back towards his car.

Before long, they reached Sam's car, and he opened the door for her with a courteous gesture. As she settled into the passenger seat, Sam couldn't shake the feeling of contentment that settled over him. He was grateful for the chance to spend more time with Natalie.

As they began driving, Sam looked for something to say to pass the time.

"So, tell me about your family," Sam prompted, glancing over at Natalie with genuine interest.

Natalie smiled warmly, her eyes lighting up as she spoke. "We're a family with a strong sense of social justice," she replied, a hint of pride in her voice. "My parents have always been activists, and my siblings and I have followed in their footsteps."

"That's admirable," Sam commented, genuinely impressed. "What kind of activism are they involved in?"

Natalie's smile widened. "Well, my older brother is a community organizer, and my younger sister, Anida, is deeply involved in the civil rights movement. She's been working tirelessly to fight for equality and justice for all."

"Wow, that's incredible," Sam marveled, inspired by Anida's dedication. "It sounds like you come from a family that's making a real difference in the world."

Natalie shook her head in agreement, a sense of pride evident in her voice. "We believe in using our voices to stand up for what's right," she explained. "And Anida's passion for the civil rights movement has always been inspiring to me."

As they continued to chat about Natalie's family and their commitment to social justice, Sam gained a deeper appreciation for the woman beside him. He admired her family's unwavering dedication to fighting for equality and felt a sense of admiration for their shared values.

Before long, they arrived at Natalie's house, and Sam reluctantly pulled to a stop outside. As she thanked him for the ride, Sam couldn't help but feel grateful for the glimpse into Natalie's life and the opportunity to learn more about the person she was.

As she disappeared inside her house with a wave and a smile, Sam couldn't help but feel excited about the prospect of future conversations and the chance to continue getting to know her better.

As Sam drove back home, his mind was filled with thoughts of Natalie. The memory of their conversation lingered in his thoughts, bringing a smile to his lips as he recalled the easy rapport they had shared. He couldn't help but feel a sense of warmth at the memory of her laughter, her bright eyes, and the genuine connection they had formed during their time together.

As he navigated the familiar streets of his neighborhood, Sam found himself replaying their conversation in his mind, savoring each moment as if it were a cherished memory. He couldn't deny the spark of excitement that had ignited within him during their time together, the sense of anticipation for the possibility of future conversations and shared moments.

Lost in thought, Sam found himself smiling as he pulled into his driveway. The evening air was cool against his skin, but inside, he felt a warmth that had nothing to do with the temperature. It was the warmth of connection, of shared laughter and meaningful conversation, and it filled him with a sense of contentment that he hadn't felt in a long time.

Entering his house, Sam was greeted by the comforting scent of home cooking and the familiar sight of his mother bustling about in the kitchen. She turned to him with a warm smile as he walked in.

"Hey, Mom," Sam greeted her, returning her smile. "My day off was pretty good, actually. I spent it with a friend."

His mother raised an eyebrow, her smile turning mischievous. "A friend, huh? Is it a girl?"

Sam felt a flush of embarrassment creeping up his neck at the teasing tone in his mother's voice. He couldn't help but chuckle nervously as he replied, "Yeah, her name's Natalie. We just went for a drive and hung out for a bit."

His mother's smile softened, her eyes twinkling with amusement. "Well, it's nice to hear you're spending time with friends, regardless of gender," she said, her tone gentle. "Natalie sounds lovely. Maybe you'll bring her by sometime so we can meet her."

Sam smiled inside, feeling a sense of relief at his mother's supportive response. "Yeah, maybe," he agreed, grateful for her understanding. "We'll see."

With a final smile, Sam headed off to his room, feeling a sense of warmth and acceptance wash over him. He knew he was lucky to have a mother who supported him, no matter who his friends were, and he felt a surge of gratitude for the unconditional love she always showed him.

As Sam prepared his uniform for the next day's shift, a contented smile played on his lips. Instead of dwelling on the work day ahead, his thoughts were consumed by memories of his time with Natalie. He found himself folding his uniform with a sense of lightness in his heart, the anticipation of seeing her again bringing a newfound excitement to his evening routine.

With each neatly pressed shirt and polished badge, Sam's mind drifted back to the conversations they had shared, the laughter that had filled the air, and the easy camaraderie that had blossomed between them. He couldn't help but feel a surge of happiness at the thought of spending more time with Natalie, knowing that their connection was something special.

As he carefully arranged his gear, Sam couldn't shake the feeling of anticipation that bubbled within him. He found himself looking forward to the next day's shift, not because of the work itself, but because it meant another chance to see Natalie, to continue building their friendship, and to see where their connection might lead.

With his uniform neatly laid out and his thoughts still filled with Natalie's smile, Sam retired for the evening, feeling a sense of contentment and excitement for the day to come. And as he drifted off to sleep, he couldn't help but feel grateful for the unexpected joy that Natalie had brought into his life.

Chapter 5
Trial By Fire

THE MORNING SUNLIGHT rushes gently through the curtains of Sam's bedroom as he stirs from sleep. As he blinks away the remnants of dreams, his thoughts immediately drift to Natalie, her image vivid in his mind's eye. He can't help but smile as he recalls their time together, the easy banter and shared laughter filling him with a sense of warmth and contentment.

With a stretch and a yawn, Sam rises from bed and pads across the room to the window, drawing back the curtains to greet the new day. The air is crisp and invigorating, carrying with it the promise of possibility and adventure. As he takes a moment to savor the quiet calm of the morning, his thoughts drift back to Natalie, her presence lingering like a sweet fragrance in the air.

As he moves through his morning routine—showering, shaving, and dressing for the day ahead—Sam finds himself humming a tune under his breath, the melody a reflection of the lightness he feels in his heart. He can't shake the feeling of anticipation that fills him, the sense that today will be different somehow, filled with unexpected twists and turns.

With a final glance in the mirror, Sam straightens his uniform and gathers his belongings, a smile tugging at the corners of his lips.

Sam arrives at the Pineworth Police Department, the familiar sight of the imposing building standing tall against the morning sky. As he steps out of his car, he takes a moment to pause and survey his surroundings, the bustle of activity around him a stark contrast to the peacefulness of his morning drive.

The air is alive with the sound of voices, the chatter of fellow officers mingling with the occasional blare of a siren in the distance. Sam feels a sense of camaraderie wash over him as he exchanges nods and greetings with his colleagues, a feeling of belonging settling in his chest.

As Sam makes his way towards the briefing room, he notices his friend Jordan approaching with a young man in tow. Jordan's easy smile and jovial demeanor never fail to lift Sam's spirits, and today is no exception.

"Hey, Sam!" Jordan calls out, a grin spreading across his face. "Got someone I want you to meet."

Sam turns to see Jordan gesturing towards the young man beside him, a slight figure with a determined expression and a hint of nervousness in his eyes. Sam extends a hand in greeting, his own smile widening as he takes in the sight of the newest addition to the force.

"Nice to meet you," Sam says warmly, shaking the young man's hand. "I'm Sam Anderson."

The young man returns the handshake with a firm grip, his gaze steady as he meets Sam's eyes. "Jamal Brown," he replies, his voice steady despite the nerves. "Pleasure to meet you, Officer Anderson."

Sam can't help but feel a surge of pride at the sight of Jamal, an African American officer in a department that has long been lacking in diversity. He knows that Jamal's presence is a sign of progress, a step towards a more inclusive and representative police force.

"It's great to see some new blood around here," Sam says, nodding towards Jamal. "Welcome aboard."

Jordan chuckles, clapping Jamal on the back with a grin. "Watch out, Sam," he jokes. "This kid's a real go-getter. Wouldn't be surprised if he ended up being chief one day."

Sam laughs, a sense of camaraderie filling the air as they continue towards the briefing room. Despite the seriousness of the situation unfolding at the civil rights rally, Sam can't help but feel a sense of optimism for the future, knowing that officers like Jamal are leading the way toward positive change within the department.

Sam laughs, a sense of camaraderie filling the air as they continue towards the briefing room.

As Sam, Jordan, and Jamal enter the briefing room, they find Chief Johnson standing at the front, his expression serious as he addresses the assembled officers. Sam takes a seat, his attention entirely focused on the chief as he begins to speak.

"Good morning, everyone," Chief Johnson starts, his voice commanding the attention of the room. "I have an important announcement to make regarding the upcoming school year."

The room falls silent as Chief Johnson continues, his words carrying a heavy weight in the air.

"We have received intel that a group opposed to the integration of schools is planning a

peaceful protest at the high school today," he says, his tone grave. "We've been assured that it will be peaceful, but I want everyone to be on high alert. The last thing we want is for things to escalate."

Sam feels a knot form in his stomach when he hears the news. The prospect of tension and potential conflict weighs heavily on his mind, and he exchanges a worried glance with Jordan and Jamal. He knows that they will need to be vigilant, keep a close eye on the situation, and ensure that it doesn't spiral out of control.

Chief Johnson's voice pulls Sam from his thoughts as he outlines the plan for the day. "I want all officers to be stationed around the high school perimeter," he instructs. "Keep an eye out for any signs of trouble, and be prepared to intervene if necessary. Our priority is to keep the peace and ensure the safety of all students and staff as there will be people on campus for opening house."

As Chief Johnson finishes his briefing, Jordan, ever the joker, can't resist adding a bit of levity to the solemn atmosphere. With a mischievous grin, he quips, "Well, Chief, if we keep patrolling schools, pretty soon we'll all be fighting over who gets to be class president."

The room erupts into laughter at Jordan's jest, the tension easing as the officers enjoy the moment of shared humor. Chief Johnson's response is quick and sharp, but there's a twinkle of amusement in his eyes as he shoots back, "Keep joking like that, Jordan, and you'll be demoted to hall monitor duty."

More laughter follows, and Sam finds himself joining in, grateful for the brief respite from the weight of the situation they're facing. It's moments like these, the camaraderie and banter among colleagues, that help to strengthen the bonds between them and keep morale high, even in the face of adversity.

As the laughter subsides and the room quiets down, Sam can't help but feel a sense of solidarity among his fellow officers. Whatever challenges may come their way, he knows they'll face them together, united in their commitment to keeping their community safe.

As Sam arrives at his post in the parking lot of the high school, he surveys the area with a sense of vigilance. The sun hangs high in the sky, casting a warm glow over the rows of cars parked neatly in their spaces. Students mill about, their laughter and chatter filling the air with a sense of youthful energy.

Sam adjusts his uniform, his gaze sweeping over the crowd as he searches for any signs of trouble. He knows that tensions are running high today, and he's determined to keep a close eye on the situation, ready to spring into action at a moment's notice.

As he patrols the perimeter of the parking lot, Sam's senses are on high alert, every sound and movement catching his attention. He exchanges nods and greetings with fellow officers

stationed nearby, a silent reminder of the united front they present in the face of potential unrest.

Despite the seriousness of their mission, Sam can't help but feel a sense of pride as he stands watch over the high school grounds. This is his community, his home, and he's determined to do whatever it takes to keep it safe.

About an hour goes by as Sam watches from his post in the parking lot of the high school, his attention is drawn to a fleet of cars pulling up one by one. With a sinking feeling in his gut, he realizes that these must be the protestors he was warned about. He can feel the tension in the air mounting as people begin to emerge from their vehicles, brandishing signs with slogans like "We Want Our Schools to Stay the Same" and "No to Integration."

Sam's jaw tightens as he watches the scene unfold before him. He knows that these people have a right to peacefully protest, as Chief Johnson had made clear during the briefing. But the message on their signs fills him with a sense of unease, a reminder of the deep-seated divisions that still exist within their community.

Sam squares his shoulders and focuses his attention on the crowd, his eyes scanning for any signs of trouble. He knows that his job is to keep the peace, to ensure that this protest remains civil and non-violent.

As the protestors begin to gather in the front parking lot, their voices rising in unison, Sam remains on high alert. He watches their every move with intensity, ready to intervene at the first sign of trouble.

As the minutes tick by, the protest shows no signs of escalating into violence. The crowd remains vocal but peaceful, their voices echoing off the walls of the high school as they make their message heard.

From his vantage point in the parking lot, Sam had been cautiously optimistic as the peaceful protest unfolded before him. The signs waved by the demonstrators had seemed harmless enough from a distance, their chants echoing through the air like distant thunder. It was a scene he had hoped would set a positive tone for the day—a beacon of civility in a time of uncertainty.

But then, in an instant, everything changed.

As the family of African Americans pulled into the parking lot, Sam's stomach churned with unease. He could feel the tension in the air crackling like electricity, a palpable sense of fear and hostility hanging thick over the scene.

And then, the moment of horror he had dreaded came to pass.

A rock, hurled with violent force, smashed through the back window of the family's car, shattering the fragile peace that had briefly settled over the parking lot. The sound of breaking glass reverberated through the air, a harsh reminder of the hatred and bigotry that lurked just beneath the surface of their community.

Sam's heart pounded in his chest as he raced towards the scene, his mind racing with a mix of anger and determination. He knew that he had to act quickly before the situation spiraled out of control and innocent lives were put at risk.

As he reached the family's car, he could see the shock and fear etched on their faces, their eyes wide with disbelief. Without hesitation, Sam sprang into action, his hands reaching out to check for injuries, his voice a steady anchor in the storm of chaos.

"Are you all right?" he asked, his tone firm but gentle. "Is anyone hurt?"

The family shook their heads, their voices trembling as they assured him that they were unharmed. Relief flooded through Sam, mingled with a surge of anger at the senseless violence that had unfolded before his eyes.

With a quick glance around, Sam reached for his radio, his fingers fumbling slightly with the controls as he called for backup. He knew that he couldn't handle this alone—that he needed reinforcements to ensure the safety of everyone involved.

"Dispatch, this is Officer Anderson," he said, his voice steady despite the turmoil raging within him. "We have a situation at the high school parking lot. I need backup immediately."

As Jordan and Officer Brown arrived on the scene, Sam filled them in on what had transpired, his voice tight with emotion as he recounted the events that had unfolded before his eyes.

"Did you see who threw the rock?" Jordan asked, his brow furrowed with concern.

Sam shook his head, his heart heavy with disappointment. "No," he admitted. "I just saw it coming from the crowd."

Jordan sighed, his expression grim. "Without knowing who threw it, we can't make any arrests," he said, his tone regretful but firm. "Let's just focus on moving them off the property for now."

Sam's heart sank at Jordan's words, a knot of frustration tightening in his chest. He had wanted nothing more than to see justice served for the family who had been targeted by the cowardly act of violence. But deep down, he knew that Jordan was right. Without concrete evidence, they couldn't take any further action.

Reluctantly, Sam agreed, his shoulders slumping with defeat. It pained him to admit it, but he knew that they had to prioritize the safety of everyone involved. Sometimes, justice had to take a backseat to pragmatism.

As they worked together to disperse the protestors from the property, Sam couldn't shake the feeling of disappointment that lingered within him. He had hoped that today would be a turning point, a step towards a more just and equitable society. But as he watched the crowd dissipate, he couldn't help but feel a sense of disillusionment at the harsh reality of their world.

As the night wore on and his shift drew to a close, Sam found himself lost in thought, the events of the day weighing heavily on his mind. He had done his best to maintain order and keep the peace, but deep down, he couldn't shake the feeling of frustration and disappointment that gnawed at him.

As he made his way back to the station, Jordan approached him with a sympathetic expression, his voice gentle as he spoke. "You did the right thing back there, Sam," he said, his tone reassuring. "Getting the protestors off the property was the right call. When they committed that act of violence, they forfeited their right to be considered a peaceful protest."

Sam was grateful for Jordan's words of support. He knew that his friend was right—that their primary responsibility as officers was to ensure the safety of everyone involved. But despite his agreement, a sense of unease still lingered within him.

"I just wish I could have done more," Sam admitted, his voice tinged with regret. "I blame myself for not paying closer attention, for not being able to find the one who threw the rock."

Jordan placed a comforting hand on Sam's shoulder, his gaze steady and reassuring. "You did everything you could, Sam," he said, his voice firm and convictional. "Sometimes, despite our best efforts, we can't control every outcome. But what matters is that we continue to learn and grow from our experiences, to become better officers and better people."

Jordan's words of reassurance washed over Sam like a balm for his troubled soul, offering a glimmer of solace in the midst of his self-doubt. As they stood together in the quiet of the station, Sam felt a weight lift from his shoulders, replaced by a renewed sense of resolve and purpose.

"You're right, Jordan," Sam replied, his voice steady with newfound determination. "I'll keep that in mind. Thanks, buddy."

Jordan offered him a warm smile, a silent acknowledgment of their shared understanding. "Anytime, Sam," he said, his tone filled with genuine sincerity. "We're in this together, remember?"

With a nod of gratitude, Sam bid Jordan farewell, watching as his friend headed off to continue his own duties. As he stood alone in the dimly lit corridor, Sam couldn't help but feel a sense of gratitude for the unwavering support of his fellow officer. In a profession fraught with challenges and uncertainties, having someone like Jordan by his side was a comfort beyond measure.

With a deep breath, Sam turned and made his way towards the exit, his mind already shifting towards the challenges that lay ahead. But as he stepped out into the cool night air, he felt a renewed sense of purpose coursing through his veins. Whatever obstacles may come his way, he knew that he wouldn't face them alone—not as long as he had friends like Jordan by his side.

Chapter 6
A Like-Minded Encounter

SAM'S DAY BEGAN LIKE any other, with the early morning sun glowing over the sleepy streets of Pineworth. As he climbed into his patrol car and set out on his rounds, he could already sense that it was leaning towards being a busy day.

The radio crackled to life with reports of various incidents—noise complaints, traffic violations, and the occasional domestic disturbance. Each call demanded his attention, pulling him in different directions and testing his resolve.

Despite the hectic pace, Sam remained focused and determined, his experience guiding him as he navigated the challenges of his job. He tried his best to respond to each call with professionalism and efficiency, never wavering in his commitment to serving and protecting the community he loved.

But as the morning wore on and the calls continued to come in, Sam couldn't shake the feeling of exhaustion that settled over him. The constant stream of incidents had left him feeling drained and weary, his mind racing with thoughts of what the day still held in store.

As Sam sat down to grab a quick bite to eat after responding to his latest call, his radio crackled to life with an urgent message. It was a call to respond to Jimmy Winters' home regarding a theft of farm equipment.

Setting aside his half-eaten sandwich, Sam's instincts kicked into high gear. He quickly grabbed his keys and headed out to his patrol car, his mind racing with thoughts of what he might encounter at Jimmy's farm.

When Sam arrives at Jimmy Winters' house, he finds Jimmy standing outside, looking visibly distressed. Sam approached him with a sympathetic expression, ready to conduct his investigation.

"Hey, Jimmy," Sam greeted him, his tone gentle yet authoritative. "I'm sorry to hear about what happened. Can you tell me what you saw?"

Jimmy sighed heavily, his shoulders slumping with weariness as he recounted the events of the theft. "I was out in the fields this morning, checking on the crops," he began, his voice tinged with frustration. "When I came back to the barn, I noticed that the lock had been broken and some of my equipment was missing."

Sam listened attentively, jotting down notes as Jimmy spoke. "Do you have any idea who might have done this?" he asked, his voice steady as he pressed for more information.

Jimmy shook his head, his expression grim. "I can't say for sure," he admitted. "But there have been some strangers hanging around the area lately. Could be anyone, really."

Sam made a mental note of Jimmy's observation, his mind already racing with thoughts of potential suspects. "Did you notice anything suspicious before the theft occurred?" he asked, probing for any additional details that might help in the investigation.

Jimmy paused, his brow furrowed in thought. "Well, now that you mention it," he said slowly, "I did see a couple of unfamiliar trucks driving past the farm earlier this morning. Didn't think much of it at the time, but now..."

Sam jotted down the information. "Alright, Jimmy, I'll do everything I can to track down your stolen equipment," he assured him, his tone firm and determined. "In the meantime, try to keep an eye out for anything else suspicious."

As Sam prepared to leave the scene, Jimmy approached him with a concerned expression. "Hey, Sam," he said softly, "I appreciate everything you're doing to help. It means a lot to me and my family."

Sam offered Jimmy a reassuring smile. "Of course, Jimmy. We're here to support you through this," he replied, his voice filled with sincerity. "If you need anything else, don't hesitate to reach out."

Jimmy appeared grateful, but then his expression grew somber. "I miss your grandfather, you know," he said quietly, his voice tinged with nostalgia. "He was my best friend, and we had some great times together."

Sam's heart swelled with emotion at Jimmy's words. He had always known that his grandfather was well-respected in the community, but hearing Jimmy speak so fondly of him only reinforced the depth of their bond.

Jimmy's son Henry emerged from the house, his expression curious as he approached. Jimmy greeted him warmly and then turned to Sam. "Sam," Jimmy said, gesturing toward Henry, "This is my son, Henry."

Sam offered Henry a friendly smile. "Nice to meet you, Henry," he said warmly, extending his hand in greeting.

Henry shook Sam's hand firmly, a hint of surprise crossing his features. "Same," he replied, his voice tinged with curiosity. "So, you're John Anderson's grandson, huh?"

Sam's smile widened at the mention of his grandfather. "That's right," he confirmed.

As they exchanged pleasantries, Jimmy's expression softened with reminiscence as he turned to Henry. "You know, Sam," he began, his voice tinged with nostalgia, "When Henry here was just a toddler, your grandfather John used to come over all the time. He'd spend hours playing with Henry, reading him stories, and teaching him all sorts of things."

Henry's eyes lit up with recognition at the mention of his childhood memories. "Yeah, I remember," he said, a fond smile playing on his lips. "John was like a grandfather to me too. He always had a way of making me laugh and teaching me new things."

Sam's heart swelled with pride and warmth at the mention of his grandfather's impact on Henry's life. "I'm glad to hear that," he said sincerely, his voice filled with gratitude. "He had a gift for connecting with people, and I'm proud to hear that he made such a positive impression on you, Henry."

Jimmy waved his head in agreement, his eyes misting with emotion. "Your grandfather was a special man, Sam," he said quietly. "He had a way of bringing people together and making them feel like family. We miss him dearly."

"I just know John would have been a huge activist in this segregation issue going on now," Jimmy continued, his voice filled with conviction. He glanced at Sam, his eyes reflecting a deep sense of respect and admiration for Sam's grandfather.

Sam's mind drifted to memories of his grandfather's unwavering commitment to justice and equality. "You're probably right, Jimmy," he agreed, a hint of pride coloring his voice. "Grandpa always stood up for what he believed in, no matter the cost."

"Well, I better get going," Sam said, giving Jimmy and Henry a nod. "I'll keep you updated on the case."

Jimmy smiled in appreciation, a grateful look on his face. "Thank you, Sam. We really appreciate it," he said warmly.

As Sam drove back to the station, he took in the scenery along the way, the familiar sights of the small town roads unfolding before him like pages from a well-worn book.

The road stretched out before him, flanked on either side by tall trees that cast dappled shadows on the pavement below. The branches swayed gently in the breeze, their leaves rustling softly in the wind. Sunlight filtered through the canopy above, casting a warm, golden glow over the landscape.

Occasionally, he passed by quaint, clapboard houses with picket fences and neatly manicured lawns. Some of them had children playing in the front yard, their laughter carrying on the breeze. Others had elderly couples sitting on the porch, rocking gently in their chairs as they enjoyed the afternoon sun.

As he drove further into town, he passed by the local diner, its neon sign flickering to life as dusk began to fall. The aroma of freshly brewed coffee and homemade pies wafted through the air, enticing him with its comforting familiarity.

Further down the road, he passed by the town square, where the courthouse stood tall and proud, its stately columns gleaming in the fading light. A few people milled about, chatting amiably as they went about their evening errands.

As Sam pulled into the station, he spotted Officer Brown standing outside, his brow furrowed in deep concentration. Concerned, Sam approached him, noting the look of preoccupation on the young officer's face.

"Hey, Brown, everything okay?" Sam asked, his tone filled with genuine concern.

Brown looked up, startled out of his thoughts, and offered Sam a weak smile. "Hey, Sam. Yeah, I'm fine," he replied, though his tone belied his words.

Sam raised an eyebrow, sensing that something was amiss. "You sure about that? You seem a bit out of sorts," he remarked, studying Brown closely.

Brown sighed, running a hand through his hair in frustration. "Honestly, Sam, I'm just feeling overwhelmed," he admitted, his voice tinged with exhaustion. "I'm still trying to get the hang of this new job, and on top of that, my wife just had a baby."

Sam looked sympathetically, understanding the weight of Brown's responsibilities. "That's a lot to juggle," he acknowledged, offering Brown a supportive pat on the shoulder. "But you'll get through it. Just take it one step at a time, and don't be afraid to ask for help if you need it."

Brown smiled gratefully at Sam's words, his shoulders visibly relaxing at the reassurance. "Thanks, Sam. I appreciate it," he said sincerely, a hint of relief in his voice.

As Sam walked away from Brown, he couldn't shake the conversation from his mind. It had served as a stark reminder that everyone faced their own challenges, and he wasn't alone in navigating the complexities of life and duty.

Reflecting on his own experiences, Sam realized that he, too, had struggled with balancing his personal life with the demands of his role as a police officer. But seeing Brown grappling with similar issues made him realize that they were all in this together, supporting each other through the highs and lows.

Despite the weight of his own responsibilities, Sam felt a sense of gratitude for the opportunity to offer words of encouragement to Brown. He hoped that his reassurance had provided some measure of comfort to the young officer, knowing that they were all part of a tight-knit community that looked out for one another.

As Sam's shift came to a close, he found himself reflecting on the events of the day. It had been a whirlwind of activity, from handling multiple calls to engaging in heartfelt conversations with members of the community.

Thoughts of the kind words about his grandfather lingered in his mind, a poignant reminder of the legacy he carried with him. It was touching to hear how John Anderson had touched the lives of others.

And then there was Officer Brown, opening up about the challenges he faced as he adjusted to his new role and navigated the joys and responsibilities of fatherhood. Sam felt a sense of camaraderie with Brown, grateful for the opportunity to offer support and encouragement.

It had indeed been a day filled with highs and lows, moments of connection and reflection that reminded Sam of the importance of community and compassion. As he prepared to leave the station, he carried with him a renewed sense of purpose and gratitude, ready to face whatever the next day might bring. For in the midst of life's challenges, he knew that he was not alone, surrounded by the support and camaraderie of those who walked alongside him.

Chapter 7
A Day To Remember

In the heart of Pineworth, the dawn of a new day carried profound significance as the town prepared to embark on a journey unlike any before. It was the long-awaited first day of school, a day brimming with hope, apprehension, and monumental change.

For generations, Pineworth had been a town divided, its schools segregated by race, its community fractured by prejudice and fear. But today marked a pivotal moment in the town's history—a moment of reckoning and renewal as the doors of Pineworth High School swung open to students of all races and backgrounds.

The significance of this day rippled through the town, stirring emotions and igniting conversations in every corner. It was a day that held the promise of a brighter future, where the barriers of segregation would be torn down, and the seeds of unity and understanding would be planted in their place.

For many in Pineworth, the first day of integrated schooling represented a long-awaited opportunity for progress and reconciliation. It was a chance to bridge the divides that had long plagued the community and embrace diversity as a source of strength rather than division.

But for others, the prospect of integration stirred deep-seated anxieties and resistance. Change, after all, was never easy, and the road ahead was sure to be fraught with challenges and uncertainties.

It was a momentous occasion for Sam and his fellow police officers. Everyone was called in to mediate the upcoming situation.

Chief Johnson stood at the front of the room, his authoritative presence commanding the attention of everyone present. His expression was serious, reflecting the gravity of the situation they were about to face.

"Alright, everyone," Chief Johnson began, his voice steady and commanding. "I know today is no ordinary day. With the integration of Pineworth High School, we're facing uncharted territory. But I have every confidence in each and every one of you to uphold the law and ensure the safety of our community."

He paused, scanning the room with a stern gaze before continuing. "I won't sugarcoat it—there may be challenges ahead. Tensions are high, emotions are running rampant, and we need to be prepared for anything."

The officers stood in silent agreement, their expressions reflecting a mixture of determination and resolve.

"Your primary objective today is to maintain order and keep the peace," Chief Johnson emphasized. "We're here to ensure that every student, regardless of race or background, feels safe and welcome in our schools. That means zero tolerance for any acts of violence, discrimination, or intimidation."

He paused, letting his words sink in before concluding with a note of encouragement. "I know we're asking a lot of you today, but I have full faith in your abilities to rise to the occasion. Remember, we're all in this together. Let's show Pineworth what it means to serve and protect with integrity and honor."

With those final words, Chief Johnson dismissed the officers to their respective assignments, their minds focused and their resolve steeled for the challenges that lay ahead.

As Sam made his way toward the door, Chief Johnson's commanding voice halted him in his tracks. With a sense of curiosity and apprehension, Sam turned back to face his superior, his expression attentive as Chief Johnson beckoned him over.

"Sam," Chief Johnson called out, his tone carrying a gravity that immediately caught Sam's attention. "I need to speak with you for a moment."

Sam approached Chief Johnson, his heart rate quickening with anticipation. He wondered what the chief had to say, his mind racing with possibilities.

"Sam, I've been thinking," Chief Johnson began, his voice measured and serious. "With the tensions surrounding the first week of school, I've decided to put you in charge of school security."

Sam's eyes widened in surprise at the unexpected assignment. He hadn't expected to be given such a crucial responsibility, especially on such a pivotal day.

"You'll be managing the perimeter and handling any protests that occur," Chief Johnson continued, his gaze steady as he met Sam's eyes. "I trust your judgment and your ability to maintain order under pressure. This is a critical task, Sam, and I know you're up to the challenge."

As Sam walked away from the conversation with Chief Johnson, a mixture of emotions swirled within him. Gratitude mingled with frustration, and a sense of duty warred with a longing for autonomy.

On one hand, Sam felt deeply grateful for Chief Johnson's trust in him. Being put in charge of school security during such a critical time was a testament to his skills and dedication as a police officer. He knew that this assignment came with great responsibility, and he was determined to fulfill it to the best of his abilities.

But on the other hand, a part of Sam couldn't shake the feeling of disappointment. He hadn't signed up to spend all of his time patrolling the school grounds, managing protests, and dealing with potential conflicts. He had joined the police force to serve his community in a variety of ways, not to be confined to one specific task.

However, as Sam reflected on Chief Johnson's words, he knew deep down that this was where he was needed most right now. The safety and well-being of the students and staff at Pineworth High School were paramount, and Sam understood that his role in maintaining order and security during this tumultuous time was essential.

With a heavy sigh, Sam resolved to set aside his personal feelings and focus on the task at hand. He may not have chosen this assignment for himself, but he was determined to make the best of it. After all, he was a police officer—a servant of the community—and that meant putting the needs of others above his own desires.

As Sam arrived at the school an hour before the start of classes, a sense of purpose infused his every step. He knew that he had been entrusted with a crucial responsibility, and he was determined to prove himself worthy of the task.

Taking charge with confidence, Sam gathered his fellow officers together and began distributing assignments with clarity and precision. He outlined their roles and responsibilities for the day, emphasizing the importance of vigilance, professionalism, and, above all, the safety of the students and staff.

With each assignment handed out, Sam made a point to offer words of encouragement and support to his colleagues. He knew that teamwork would be essential in ensuring the success of their mission, and he was determined to foster a spirit of unity and cooperation among his fellow officers.

As the officers dispersed to their respective posts, Sam remained behind, ready to take on the challenges of the day head-on. It was his time to lead, and he embraced the opportunity with determination and resolve.

As the other officers filed out of the high school, Sam found himself approached by a man whose presence exuded authority—the school principal, Mr. Smith. With a firm handshake and a friendly smile, Mr. Smith introduced himself, his demeanor reflecting a blend of professionalism and warmth.

"Officer Anderson, it's a pleasure to meet you," Mr. Smith greeted him, his tone respectful yet welcoming. "I'm Mr. Smith, the principal here at Pineworth High School."

Returning the handshake with equal firmness, Sam returned the sentiment, "Likewise, Mr. Smith. Thank you for having us here today."

Mr. Smith proceeded to outline his expectations for the morning, his voice carrying an air of authority tempered with understanding. He emphasized the importance of maintaining a welcoming and secure environment for the students while also ensuring that any disruptions or incidents were addressed swiftly and appropriately.

"I expect that every student who walks through these doors feels safe, respected, and supported," Mr. Smith stated firmly, his gaze meeting Sam's with unwavering determination. "We're here to provide a positive learning environment, and your presence is crucial in ensuring that goal is met."

Sam agreed, his own sense of responsibility aligning perfectly with Mr. Smith's expectations. "You can count on us, Mr. Smith," he replied, his voice filled with assurance. "We'll do everything in our power to ensure the safety and well-being of the students and staff."

As Mr. Smith relayed his instructions to Sam, the gravity of the situation weighed heavily on both of them. Sam listened intently as Mr. Smith outlined his plan, his expression thoughtful and his mind already racing with implications.

"I want all officers outside the school except for you, Officer Anderson," Mr. Smith stated firmly, his tone leaving no room for debate. "I want the students to feel like the issue is outside, not on the inside. Your presence here is important to maintain a sense of security without causing unnecessary alarm."

Sam expressed his understanding, recognizing the wisdom in Mr. Smith's approach. It was crucial to strike a delicate balance between ensuring safety and avoiding undue disruption to the school environment.

"And as for any events that occur within the school between students," Mr. Smith continued, his voice steady and resolute, "they will be handled by school personnel. We have our own procedures in place for addressing disciplinary issues, and I trust in our staff's ability to handle them appropriately."

Sam admired his way of going about his business and acknowledged Mr. Smith's authority and expertise in matters concerning the school's internal affairs. While he was prepared to intervene if necessary, he understood the importance of allowing the school to maintain its autonomy and handle its own matters whenever possible.

"Understood, Mr. Smith," Sam replied, his voice conveying his respect for the principal's decisions. "I'll ensure that our officers follow your instructions to the letter. We're here to support you and the school in any way we can."

With a nod of appreciation, Mr. Smith thanked Sam for his cooperation before turning to attend to his duties. Left alone once more, Sam felt a sense of reassurance knowing that they were all working together towards a common goal—the safety and well-being of the students and staff of Pineworth High School.

As the morning unfolded and the first wave of students and parents began to arrive at Pineworth High School, Sam found himself immersed in a scene that was both familiar and fraught with tension. The atmosphere crackled with anticipation, a palpable sense of unease lingering in the air as whispers and murmurs spread among the gathered crowd.

The school grounds buzzed with activity, students chatting excitedly with friends, parents exchanging greetings and well-wishes, and staff members bustling about in preparation for the day ahead. But beneath the surface, there was an undercurrent of apprehension—a sense of uncertainty that hung heavy in the air like a storm cloud on the horizon.

And then, as if on cue, they arrived—the protestors. A small group of individuals, their faces set in stern expressions, their voices raised in unison as they brandished signs and banners emblazoned with slogans of resistance and defiance.

The scene unfolded like a scene from a familiar script—a script that had played out in countless schools across the country grappling with the same issue. The protestors stood at the edge of the school grounds, their presence a stark reminder of the divisions that still lingered within the community.

Sam watched from his vantage point near the entrance, his eyes scanning the crowd with a mixture of vigilance and apprehension. He knew that this was a critical moment—a moment that would test the resolve of everyone involved.

The tension in the air was palpable, a thick fog of uncertainty that enveloped the school grounds like a shroud. Parents exchanged uneasy glances, students cast furtive looks at the protestors, and staff members stood ready to spring into action at a moment's notice.

But amidst the chaos and confusion, there was also a sense of determination—a quiet resolve that simmered beneath the surface, ready to ignite into action at a moment's notice. Sam felt it in the air, a silent rallying cry that whispered of solidarity and strength in the face of adversity.

As Sam scanned the bustling scene before him from his position at the front of the school, his attention was suddenly drawn to a commotion erupting further down the line. A surge of protestors, their voices raised in defiance, seemed to be pressing against a small group of officers—Jordan and Jamal.

Without a moment's hesitation, Sam sprang into action, his instincts kicking into high gear as he rushed toward the unfolding confrontation. The urgency of the situation propelled him forward, his heart pounding in his chest as he prepared to lend his support to his fellow officers.

As he drew closer, the full extent of the chaos became clear. The protestors, their faces contorted with anger and determination, were pushing against Jordan and Jamal with increasing force, their collective momentum threatening to overwhelm the two officers.

With a sense of urgency coursing through his veins, Sam waded into the fray, his presence a reassuring beacon of authority amidst the swirling sea of dissent. He positioned himself alongside Jordan and Jamal, his gaze locked on the protestors as he braced himself for whatever came next.

The air crackled with tension, the intensity of the moment palpable as the standoff reached a fever pitch. But Sam stood firm, his resolve unwavering as he faced down the protestors with unwavering determination.

Together, he and his fellow officers formed a united front, their collective strength a powerful symbol of resilience in the face of adversity.

As the last of the students trickled into the school, the protestors began to disperse, their voices fading into the distance as they retreated from the scene. But amidst the dwindling crowd, one figure remained—a lone protester, his gaze fixed unwaveringly on Sam.

Sam returned the man's stare, his expression resolute as he braced himself for whatever might come next. There was a tension in the air, a palpable sense of anticipation as the standoff between them stretched on.

Sensing the escalating tension, Jordan moved to intervene, his voice calm but firm as he approached the man. "Sir, it's time to leave," he said, his tone carrying a note of authority.

But the man didn't budge. Instead, he stood his ground, his fists clenched at his sides as he met Jordan's gaze with defiance. Sam's pulse quickened as he watched the exchange, his instincts on high alert as he prepared for any possible escalation.

As Jordan moved closer to the man, Sam's senses went into overdrive. He could see the tension in the man's body, the simmering anger beneath the surface threatening to boil over at any moment. It was a dangerous situation, and Sam knew that they needed to defuse it quickly before it spiraled out of control.

With a steely resolve, Sam stepped forward, positioning himself beside Jordan as a show of solidarity. Together, they faced down the man, their united front a powerful deterrent against any further aggression.

"Sir, we're asking you to leave peacefully," Sam said, his voice firm but measured. "There's no need for any more trouble here today."

For a moment, the man hesitated, his gaze flickering between Sam and Jordan as if weighing his options. And then, with a reluctant nod, he finally relented, turning on his heel and disappearing into the crowd.

As the tension began to dissipate, Sam felt a surge of relief wash over him. They had managed to defuse the situation without any further incident, averting a potential confrontation and ensuring the safety of everyone involved.

Chapter 8
A Break For The Mind

AS THE LAST ECHOES of the protests faded into the distance and a sense of calm settled over the school grounds, Sam breathed a sigh of relief. The dismissal had been free of further incident, much to his relief, and he couldn't help but feel a sense of gratitude that the situation had been resolved without any further escalation.

However, as he scanned the area one last time before turning to leave, his eyes caught sight of a lone figure standing off in the distance—a solitary silhouette against the backdrop of the setting sun. His heart skipped a beat as he recognized the familiar shape, and a sense of unease crept over him.

Could it be the same man from earlier in the day? The one who had lingered behind after the other protestors had dispersed? Sam couldn't be sure, but something about the figure's posture and demeanor sent a shiver down his spine.

With a sense of caution, Sam made his way toward the distant figure, his steps slow and deliberate as he approached. As he drew closer, he could see the man's features more clearly—the set of his jaw, the tension in his shoulders, the intensity of his gaze.

"Can I help you?" Sam called out, his voice carrying across the quiet expanse of the school grounds. The figure turned to face him, their eyes meeting in a silent exchange that seemed to stretch on for eternity.

For a moment, neither of them spoke, the air thick with unspoken tension. And then, with a curt nod, the figure turned and disappeared into the gathering shadows, leaving Sam alone with his thoughts and the lingering sense of unease that hung heavy in the air.

As he watched the figure retreat into the distance, Sam couldn't shake the feeling that their encounter was far from over. There was something about the way the man had looked at him—a silent challenge, a lingering threat—that left him with a nagging sense of foreboding.

As the day drew to a close and Sam's duties at the school came to an end, he found himself with a rare moment of silence. With the school secure and his responsibilities fulfilled, he decided to take advantage of the opportunity to pay a visit to Natalie.

She had been on his mind ever since their last encounter, her presence lingering in his thoughts like a gentle whisper on the breeze.

With a sense of anticipation coursing through his veins, Sam climbed into his car and set off towards Natalie's house.

With a determined resolve, Sam stepped out of his car and made his way up the path to Natalie's front door. Each step brought him closer to her, closer to the possibility of reconnecting and sharing in each other's company once more.

And as he reached out to knock on the door, a sense of anticipation washed over him.

As the door swung open, Sam found himself face to face with an elderly gentleman—the unmistakable air of authority and wisdom in his demeanor marking him as Natalie's father. With a respectful nod, Sam greeted him, his voice calm and polite as he inquired about Natalie's whereabouts.

"Good evening, sir," Sam began, his tone respectful. "Is Natalie home by any chance?"

The elderly gentleman regarded him with a knowing expression, a faint smile playing at the corners of his lips. "Yes, she is," he replied, his voice warm and welcoming. "May I ask who's calling?"

Sam hesitated for a moment, gathering his thoughts before responding. "My name is Sam," he explained, his words measured and sincere. "I'm a friend of Natalie's, and I was hoping to speak with her if possible."

The man's eyes twinkled with a hint of amusement as he regarded Sam as if sizing him up with a shrewd eye. And then, with a nod of approval, he stepped aside, gesturing for Sam to enter.

"Of course, Sam," he said, his voice tinged with a hint of paternal warmth. "Please, come in. Natalie will be delighted to see you."

With a grateful smile, Sam stepped over the threshold, his heart racing.

As Natalie's father called out to her, Sam's heart skipped a beat in anticipation. Moments later, Natalie emerged from the shadows of the staircase, her presence filling the room with a radiant warmth that stole Sam's breath away.

She wore a gentle smile on her lips, her eyes sparkling with a mixture of surprise and delight at the sight of Sam standing in her doorway. For a moment, they simply gazed at each other, the air alive with unspoken emotions that hung between them like a delicate veil.

"Sam," Natalie said, her voice soft and melodious as she approached him, her every movement graceful and elegant. "What a wonderful surprise."

Sam returned her smile, his own heart swelling with happiness at the sight of her. "Natalie," he replied, his voice filled with warmth. "It's good to see you."

Their eyes locked in a silent exchange, each one silently acknowledging the unspoken connection that bound them together. In that moment, surrounded by the comfort of Natalie's home and the gentle glow of her presence, Sam knew that he was exactly where he was meant to be.

As Natalie turned to her father, she spoke with a gentle yet determined tone, her eyes meeting his with a sense of assurance.

"Dad," she said, her voice soft but resolute, "I'll be out for a few hours. Sam and I are going to catch up."

Her father regarded her with a knowing smile, a twinkle of amusement in his eyes as he gave her a serious glance. "Of course, dear," he replied, his voice tinged with affection. "Enjoy yourselves, but be safe."

With a reassuring smile, Natalie waved goodbye in response before turning back to Sam, motioning for him to follow her outside. Sam offered a respectful nod to Natalie's father as he passed, a sense of gratitude filling him for the warm welcome he had received.

"Nice to meet you, sir," Sam said sincerely before stepping out into the cool evening air with Natalie by his side.

As Sam and Natalie embarked on their drive to the town square, the soft hum of the car engine provided a soothing backdrop to their conversation. The warm glow of streetlights illuminated the quiet streets, casting gentle shadows across the familiar landmarks that passed by in a blur.

Natalie leaned back in her seat, her eyes fixed on the passing scenery outside the window. Sam stole a glance at her from time to time, taking in the serene expression on her face, her features bathed in the soft amber light.

"So, what brought you to see me?" Natalie's question broke the comfortable silence, her voice soft and curious as she turned to look at Sam.

Sam met her gaze with a warm smile, his eyes reflecting the sincerity of his words. "I just wanted to spend some time with you," he replied honestly, his tone gentle. "I've been thinking about you a lot lately."

A faint blush colored Natalie's cheeks at his words, and she ducked her head shyly, a smile playing at the corners of her lips. "I'm glad you came," she said softly, her voice filled with warmth.

As they rounded the corner and the town square came into view, Sam felt a sense of anticipation building within him. The vibrant energy of the bustling square seemed to beckon them forward, promising endless possibilities and the chance to create new memories together.

"I'm sorry about my dad. He likes to be protective." She said.

Her words about her father brought a sympathetic smile to his lips, and he reached out to gently squeeze her hand in reassurance. "Don't worry about it," he said softly, his tone gentle. "I understand. And I'm glad we have this chance to talk, just the two of us."

As they continued to walk, the weight of the world seemed to fall away, leaving only the quiet companionship of the night and the gentle rhythm of their conversation. As they shared their thoughts and dreams with each other, Sam couldn't help but feel a sense of gratitude for the unexpected connection that had brought them together—a connection that he knew, deep down, was something truly special.

As they found a quiet spot in the town square, Natalie turned to Sam with a curious expression, her eyes reflecting genuine interest as she asked, "So, what do you want to talk about?"

Sam took a moment to gather his thoughts before responding, his gaze meeting hers with a sense of sincerity. "Well, there's been a lot on my mind lately," he began, his voice tinged with a hint of concern. "Especially with everything going on at the schools."

Natalie listened intently as Sam recounted the stress he had been feeling about the tensions surrounding the school integration, his words carrying the weight of his responsibilities as a police officer tasked with ensuring the safety of the students and faculty.

"And then there's this guy I saw," Sam continued, his brow furrowing slightly as he recalled the encounter. "He was hanging around across the street from the school during dismissal, and something about him just didn't sit right with me."

Natalie's expression softened with concern as she reached out to gently squeeze Sam's hand, her touch offering a comforting reassurance. "That sounds worrying," she said softly, her voice filled with empathy. "Is there anything I can do to help?"

Sam's heart swelled with gratitude at Natalie's offer of support, and he returned her squeeze with a grateful smile. "Just having you here to listen means a lot," he replied sincerely, his gaze meeting hers with a sense of appreciation. "Thank you for being here for me, Natalie."

As Sam shared his concerns with Natalie and felt her genuine empathy and support, a weight seemed to lift from his shoulders, replaced by a sense of relief and gratitude.

He had always been accustomed to keeping his work issues close to his chest, confiding only in his longtime friend Jordan. But there was something about Natalie's presence, her understanding gaze and comforting words, that made him feel safe enough to open up in a way he never had before.

As he spoke, Natalie listened attentively, her expression one of genuine concern and compassion. And as she offered her support and understanding, Sam felt a sense of connection and camaraderie that he had never experienced before. It was as iIf in that moment, their worlds had aligned, and he knew that no matter what challenges lay ahead, he wouldn't have to face them alone.

With a grateful smile, Sam reached out to take Natalie's hand, the warmth of her touch grounding him in the present moment. "Thank you," he said softly, his voice filled with sincerity. "I've never shared this with anyone else before, but with you...it just feels right."

Natalie returned his smile with a gentle squeeze of his hand, her eyes reflecting the depth of her understanding and support. "I'm glad you feel comfortable sharing with me," she replied softly. "You can always count on me to be here for you, Sam."

As they sat together in the quiet of the town square, the weight of Sam's worries seemed to fade into the background, replaced by a sense of comfort and reassurance that came from knowing he had someone like Natalie by his side. In that moment, Sam realized that sometimes, sharing your burdens with someone you trust can make all the difference in the world.

As Sam and Natalie continued their conversation, the topic shifted to Natalie's own life and struggles. With a thoughtful expression, Sam asked, "How are things going in your life, Natalie? Is everything alright?"

Natalie hesitated for a moment, her brow furrowing with a hint of uncertainty before she replied, "Honestly, Sam, things have been pretty stressful lately." She took a deep breath, gathering her thoughts before continuing, "I recently started working at the Pineworth ER, and while I'm grateful for the opportunity, the learning curve has been... challenging, to say the least."

Sam listened intently, his heart going out to Natalie as he recognized the familiar weight of stress and uncertainty in her words. "I'm sorry to hear that, Natalie," he said softly, reaching out to gently squeeze her hand in a gesture of solidarity. "It sounds like you've been dealing with a lot."

Natalie offered him a small, grateful smile, her eyes reflecting a mix of vulnerability and appreciation. "Yeah, it's been tough," she admitted, her voice tinged with a hint of exhaustion. "But talking to you and sharing this with someone who understands... I think I needed this as much as you did, Sam."

Sam felt a surge of empathy and understanding wash over him, a sense of connection and camaraderie blossoming between them in the quiet of the town square. "I'm glad we could be here for each other," he said sincerely, his gaze meeting Natalie's with a shared understanding. "We'll get through this together, Natalie. I promise."

As they sat together, the weight of their worries seemed to lighten, replaced by a newfound sense of companionship and support that filled the air with hope and possibility.

As Sam escorted Natalie back to her doorstep, a sense of gratitude and warmth enveloped them both, the quiet night air alive with the gentle hum of their conversation. As they reached her front door, Sam turned to face her, a soft smile playing at the corners of his lips.

"Thank you for tonight, Natalie," Sam said sincerely, his voice filled with appreciation. "I really needed this talk."

Natalie returned his smile, her eyes sparkling with a mix of emotions. "I'm glad we could talk, Sam," she replied softly, her voice tinged with sincerity. "It meant a lot to me too."

And then, without hesitation, Natalie leaned in and pressed a gentle kiss against Sam's cheek, a tender gesture filled with gratitude and affection. Sam's heart skipped a beat at the unexpected touch, warmth spreading through him at the simple yet meaningful act of kindness.

"Thank you," Natalie whispered, her voice barely above a whisper as she pulled back, her eyes meeting Sam's with a depth of emotion that left him breathless.

With a soft smile, Sam reached out to gently cup Natalie's cheek, his thumb tracing the curve of her jawline with a gentle caress. "You're welcome," he murmured, his voice barely audible above the soft rustle of the evening breeze. "Anytime."

Chapter 9
Whispers of Farewell

THE MORNING SUN ROSE lazily over Pineworth, casting long shadows that stretched across the quiet streets as Sam began his weekend shift on patrol. From the moment he stepped out of his house, a sense of unease hung heavy in the air, the usual rhythm of the day feeling somehow off-kilter.

As he drove through the familiar streets of his hometown, Sam couldn't shake the feeling of foreboding that settled over him like a dark cloud. The chirping of birds seemed muted, the vibrant colors of the buildings dulled by an invisible haze of worry that seemed to seep into every corner of the town.

Even the chatter over the police radio sounded distant and disjointed, each call blending into the next in a cacophony of noise that failed to drown out the gnawing sense of unease that gnawed at Sam's insides.

As he made his rounds, Sam couldn't help but feel as though he were moving through a world that had been cast in shadow, the usual bustle of the town replaced by a heavy silence that seemed to press down on him with every passing moment.

And as he drove, his thoughts drifted inexorably to his family, his father's declining health weighing heavily on his mind. With each passing hour, the worry that had been building inside him threatened to consume him whole, the knowledge that he was powerless to protect his loved ones from the trials of life filling him with a sense of helplessness he couldn't shake.

As Sam navigated the quiet streets of Pineworth, the crackle of the police radio broke through the stillness, pulling him from his thoughts. Dispatch's voice echoed through the car, crisp and urgent.

"Unit 12, this is dispatch. Please report to Chief Johnson's office immediately. Over."

Sam's brow furrowed in confusion, a knot of apprehension tightening in his stomach. He glanced down at the radio, a sense of unease creeping over him. He hadn't been expecting any specific instructions from Chief Johnson, and the urgency in dispatch's voice only served to heighten his anxiety.

With a furrowed brow, Sam acknowledged the message, his grip tightening on the steering wheel as he redirected his patrol car toward the police station. As he drove, questions swirled through his mind, each one more troubling than the last. What could Chief Johnson want with him? Has something happened?

Despite the reassurances he tried to offer himself, Sam couldn't shake the sense of unease that settled over him like a heavy shroud. All he could do was steel himself for whatever awaited him at Chief Johnson's office, his heart pounding with a mixture of apprehension and dread as he prepared for the unknown.

As Sam hurriedly made his way to Chief Johnson's office, a knot of worry formed in his stomach, the urgency in the chief's voice sending a shiver down his spine. He stepped into the room, his heart pounding with apprehension as he met the chief's gaze.

"Sam," Chief Johnson began his tone grave, "I've just received a call from your mother. She said your father has been taken to the hospital."

Sam's breath caught in his throat, a wave of fear crashing over him at the news. His father's health had been declining for some time now, but this sudden turn of events filled him with a sense of unease he couldn't shake.

"I need you to go to the hospital, Sam," Chief Johnson continued, his voice softening with concern. "Take all the time you need. Your family comes first."

Sam looked down for a moment, his mind racing with worry and uncertainty. Without a word, he turned on his heel and rushed out of the office, his thoughts consumed by the fear of what he might find at the hospital.

The wail of sirens pierced the air as Sam's patrol car tore through the streets of Pineworth, his heart pounding in his chest with each passing moment. Fear clawed at his insides, threatening to overwhelm him as he raced towards the hospital, his mind consumed by worry for his father.

As he skidded to a stop in the parking lot, Sam flung open the door and leaped out of the car, his breath coming in ragged gasps as he sprinted towards the entrance. And there, standing at the doors of the hospital, was Natalie, her face etched with sorrow, and his mother, her eyes brimming with tears.

Their somber expressions said it all, sending a chill down Sam's spine as he approached them, his heart heavy with dread. Without a word, they enveloped him in a tight embrace, offering what little comfort they could in the face of such uncertainty.

Sam's stomach churned with a sickening mixture of fear and anguish as he looked between them, his throat tight with emotion. He didn't need to ask what had happened – the sorrow written on their faces spoke volumes, crushing him beneath the weight of their shared grief.

Together, they made their way into the hospital, each step heavier than the last as they braced themselves for the news that awaited them. As they entered the sterile confines of the waiting room, Sam couldn't help but pray that his father would pull through, his heart aching with the desperate hope that their beloved patriarch would emerge from this ordeal unscathed.

Sam's voice trembled as he turned to Natalie, his eyes clouded with tears. "How... how bad is it?" he managed to choke out, his heart pounding in his chest.

Natalie reached out, gently placing a hand on his shoulder. "I'm so sorry, Sam," she murmured softly. "Your father... he's in critical condition. The doctors think it might have been a heart attack, and... and they're doing everything they can, but..." Her voice trailed off, the unspoken words hanging heavy in the air.

Sam felt a lump form in his throat as he struggled to hold back his tears. "But what?" he whispered hoarsely, his voice barely above a whisper.

Natalie's eyes brimmed with tears as she met his gaze. "But they're not sure if he's going to make it," she admitted, her voice thick with emotion. "I'm so sorry, Sam. I wish there was more I could say, more I could do..."

Sam's world seemed to tilt on its axis as Natalie's words washed over him, each syllable heavy with the weight of impending loss. He felt as though the ground had dropped out from beneath him, leaving him adrift in a sea of uncertainty and despair.

A strangled gasp escaped his lips as he struggled to process the gravity of the situation, his heart constricting with a pain unlike anything he had ever known. The mere thought of losing his father sent a shiver down his spine, leaving him trembling with fear and sorrow.

Natalie's voice seemed to echo in the sterile confines of the hospital, her words ringing in his ears like a haunting refrain. He turned to her, his eyes pleading for some shred of hope amidst the darkness that threatened to engulf him.

But there was no comfort to be found in her somber gaze, only the cold, hard truth of their reality. His father's life hung in the balance, teetering on the edge of oblivion, and there was nothing they could do but wait and pray for a miracle.

With a heavy heart, Sam sank into a nearby chair, his mind swirling with a jumble of emotions. Fear, grief, and helplessness gnawed at him from within, each one threatening to consume him whole.

And as he sat there, lost in his own turmoil, Sam couldn't help but feel a profound sense of gratitude for Natalie's presence by his side. In the midst of his darkest hour, she was a beacon of light, offering him solace and support when he needed it most.

Sam shook his head, his heart aching with a pain unlike anything he had ever known. "No, Natalie, you've done enough," he said, his voice filled with gratitude. "Just... just being here with me, it means everything."

Natalie led Sam and his mother down the sterile hospital corridors, their footsteps echoing against the linoleum floors as they made their way to his father's room. Sam's heart felt heavy in his chest, each step bringing him closer to the unknown fate that awaited them.

As they reached the doorway, Natalie paused, her hand resting on the handle as she turned to Sam and his mother with a sympathetic smile. "He's resting now," she said softly. "But you can go in and sit with him for a while."

Sam opened his mouth to say okay, but nothing came out. His throat was tight with emotion as he followed Natalie into the room. His father lay in the hospital bed, his face pale and drawn, his breaths shallow and labored. Sam's heart clenched at the sight, a lump forming in his throat as he approached the bedside.

His mother took his father's hand in hers, her eyes brimming with tears as she leaned in to whisper words of love and encouragement. Sam stood by her side, his own emotions threatening to overwhelm him as he watched his father's chest rise and fall with each strained breath.

Natalie hovered nearby, her presence a comforting presence in the midst of their shared grief. Together, they stood vigil at his father's bedside, offering what little solace they could in the face of his suffering.

A flicker of awareness crossed his father's face, his eyes fluttering open for a brief moment. Sam's heart leaped in his chest at the sight, a surge of hope coursing through him as he leaned in closer, desperate to hear his father's voice once more.

"Hey, Dad," Sam said softly, his voice trembling with emotion as he reached out to grasp his father's hand. "It's me, Sam."

His father's gaze drifted towards him, a faint smile tugging at the corners of his lips. "Sam," he murmured, his voice barely above a whisper. "I'm... I'm so glad you're here."

Tears welled up in Sam's eyes as he struggled to find the words to express the depth of his love and gratitude. "I'm here, Dad," he whispered, his voice thick with emotion. "I'm right here."

His father's hand tightened around his, a silent reassurance of their unbreakable bond. "I'm... I'm sorry, Sam," he said, his voice barely audible above the soft hum of the machines surrounding them. "I'm sorry for... for everything."

Sam's heart clenched at his father's words, a flood of memories washing over him as he recalled the moments they had shared together over the years. "It's okay, Dad," he said, his voice choked with tears. "I forgive you. I always have."

His father's eyes brimmed with tears as he squeezed Sam's hand tightly. "Thank you, son," he whispered, his voice filled with a mix of sorrow and gratitude. "Thank you for... for being the best son a father could ask for."

Sam could barely speak through the lump in his throat as he leaned in to embrace his father, holding him close as tears streamed down his cheeks.

As Sam and his mother held his father's hands, a sense of quiet acceptance settled over the room, their shared grief mingling with a profound sense of love and loss. His father's breathing grew shallower with each passing moment, his chest rising and falling in a rhythm that seemed to echo the final beats of his fading heart.

With tears streaming down her cheeks, Sam's mother leaned in close, pressing a gentle kiss to his father's forehead as she whispered words of love and farewell. "Goodbye, my love," she murmured, her voice trembling with emotion. "Thank you for... for everything."

His father's eyes fluttered open for one last time, a faint smile gracing his lips as he met her gaze with a look of profound gratitude. "Thank you, my dear," he whispered, his voice barely a whisper. "For... for giving me a lifetime of love and happiness."

And with those final words, his father's breathing grew still, his chest falling silent as the last vestiges of life slipped away. Sam's heart felt as though it had shattered into a million pieces as he watched his father slip away, his hand clasped tightly on his own as he whispered a silent farewell to the man who had shaped his life in ways too numerous to count.

In that solemn moment, surrounded by the hushed stillness of the hospital room and the gentle embrace of his family, Sam felt a profound sense of loss wash over him, a deep ache that seemed to pierce his very soul. But amidst the pain and sorrow, there was also a glimmer of peace, a quiet assurance that his father's spirit would live on in the hearts of those who loved him, forever cherished and forever remembered.

As the evening settled in, casting a soft glow over the quiet neighborhood, Sam found himself sitting alone on the porch, the weight of grief heavy upon his shoulders. The rhythmic creak of the rocking chair beneath him provided a comforting cadence as he stared out into the gathering dusk, lost in his thoughts.

A gentle breeze rustled through the trees, carrying with it the faint scent of flowers and the distant murmur of life beyond the confines of his home. In the stillness of the evening, Sam felt a sense of solace wash over him, a quiet reassurance that even in the midst of sorrow, there was still beauty to be found in the world.

As he sat lost in contemplation, the sound of footsteps approaching caught his attention, drawing his gaze toward the figure making their way up the path toward his porch. It was Natalie, her expression soft and sympathetic as she approached, her presence a welcome comfort in the midst of his grief.

"Hey, Sam," she said softly, her voice carrying a gentle warmth as she settled onto the porch beside him. "I heard about your dad. I'm so sorry."

Sam offered her a faint smile, grateful for her presence in his time of need. "Thank you, Natalie," he replied, his voice tinged with emotion. "It means a lot."

They sat in companionable silence for a while, the quiet of the evening wrapping around them like a blanket as they shared their memories and thoughts of his father. In Natalie's presence, Sam felt a sense of peace settles over him, a reminder that even in the darkest moments, there were still rays of light to guide him through the storm.

Chapter 10

In Memoriam

As the morning sun rose over Pineworth, casting a golden hue over the sleepy town, Sam awoke to the somber reality of the day ahead. Today was the day of his father's funeral, a day that would mark the final farewell to a beloved patriarch and a pillar of their community.

With a heavy heart, Sam dressed in his somber black suit, each button a reminder of the solemn occasion that awaited him. The air felt heavy with grief as he made his way downstairs, where his mother was already preparing for the day ahead, her eyes red-rimmed from tears shed in the quiet hours of the morning.

Together, they made their way to the small church where the service would be held, their footsteps echoing in the empty streets as they navigated the familiar path that had become so fraught with sorrow. As they entered the hallowed halls of the church, Sam felt a sense of reverence wash over him, the weight of the moment settling like a heavy shroud upon his shoulders.

The pews were filled with mourners, their faces etched with lines of grief and sorrow as they came together to pay their final respects to a man who had touched so many lives with his kindness and compassion. Sam's heart swelled with pride as he looked upon the sea of faces gathered in remembrance of his father, a testament to the legacy he had left behind.

As the service began, Sam found himself lost in the comforting embrace of hymns and prayers, the words washing over him like a balm for his weary soul. Each eulogy and tribute served as a poignant reminder of the impact his father had made on the lives of those around him, a beacon of light in a world often darkened by hardship and despair.

One eulogy really stood out to Sam.

Jimmy Winters, a weathered farmer and longtime friend of Ronnie's, stood before the assembled crowd, his voice steady despite the weight of grief that hung heavy in the air.

"Today, we come together to honor the memory of a man who was more than just a neighbor or a friend," Jimmy began, his eyes scanning the faces of those gathered. "Ronnie Anderson was a beacon of light in our community, a guiding force who touched the lives of all who knew him."

As Jimmy spoke, memories flooded his mind, memories of long days spent working the land alongside Ronnie, the sun beating down on their backs as they labored side by side. He spoke of Ronnie's unwavering dedication to his craft, his hands calloused from years of toil, yet always quick to offer assistance to those in need.

"But Ronnie was more than just a farmer," Jimmy continued, his voice tinged with emotion. "He was a man of integrity, compassion, and unwavering faith. He lived his life with purpose and conviction, his actions speaking volumes about the kind of man he was."

Turning his gaze to Ronnie's wife, Mary, and their son, Sam, Jimmy spoke of the love and devotion that had defined Ronnie's life. "To Mary, Ronnie was a devoted partner, a source of strength and support through every trial and tribulation. And to Sam, he was not just a father but a guiding light, imparting wisdom and instilling values that would shape the man he would become."

As Jimmy concluded his eulogy, a hush fell over the crowd, broken only by the soft rustle of leaves in the gentle breeze. "Though Ronnie may no longer walk among us," Jimmy said, his voice filled with quiet reverence, "his spirit lives on in the memories we hold dear and the lives he touched. He may be gone, but his legacy will endure as a beacon of hope and inspiration for generations to come."

And with those words, Jimmy stepped back, allowing the community to come together in silent remembrance of a man whose presence would be deeply missed but whose memory would live on in the hearts of all who knew and loved him.

As the final notes of the funeral hymn echoed through the hallowed halls of the church, Sam rose to his feet, his heart heavy with sorrow yet buoyed by the knowledge that his father's spirit would live on in the hearts of those who loved him. With tears streaming down his cheeks, he joined the mourners in procession, following his father's casket to its final resting place beneath the shade of a towering oak tree, where he would be laid to rest alongside generations of ancestors who had gone before him.

As the earth closed over his father's grave, Sam felt a profound sense of loss wash over him, the weight of grief pressing down upon him like a leaden weight. But amidst the sorrow, there was also a glimmer of hope, a quiet assurance that his father's spirit would live on in the memories of those who had been touched by his love and kindness.

And as he stood in silent vigil beside his father's final resting place, Sam whispered a silent farewell to the man who had shaped his life in ways too numerous to count, grateful for the time they had shared and the memories they had created together.

As Sam and his mother stood together, accepting condolences from friends, neighbors, and acquaintances alike, the small town of Pineworth came together in a display of communal support and solidarity.

First to approach them was Natalie, her eyes glistening with unshed tears as she offered her heartfelt condolences to Sam and his mother. Her presence was a source of comfort amidst the sea of sorrow, a reminder that they were not alone in their grief.

Next came Jordan, his stoic facade crumbling as he embraced Sam in a tight hug. Words seemed inadequate in the face of such profound loss, but the silent solidarity between the two men spoke volumes, a testament to the strength of their bond.

From the back of the crowd emerged Jimmy Winters. With a weathered hand and a solemn nod, he offered his condolences to Sam and his mother, his eyes reflecting the shared sorrow that hung heavy in the air.

"Thank you, Jimmy," Sam said, his voice soft but sincere. "Your words meant a great deal to me, to my family, and to everyone who loved my father."

Jimmy looked up, his weathered face softened by a gentle smile. "Ronnie was a good man, Sam. He touched the lives of so many, mine included. It was an honor to speak on his behalf today."

Sam reached out, clasping Jimmy's rough hand in his own. "Your friendship meant the world to him, Jimmy. And it means the world to me now."

They stood there for a moment, two souls bound by grief and gratitude, finding solace in each other's presence amidst the pain of loss.

"Take care, Sam," Jimmy said, his voice filled with quiet understanding. "And if you ever need anything, you know where to find me."

With a nod of appreciation, Sam bid Jimmy farewell, grateful for the support of a friend during a time of profound sorrow.

As the day wore on, more faces from Sam's past and present came forward to offer their support, each one a reminder of the impact his father had made on the lives of those around him. Whether through a simple gesture or a heartfelt embrace, each condolence offered a small measure of solace in the midst of their grief.

And as the sun dipped below the horizon, casting long shadows across the cemetery where Sam's father now lay at rest, the community of Pineworth stood united in their collective sorrow, bound together by the ties of love and friendship that would endure long after the final words of condolence had been spoken.

After the funeral, Sam drove through the winding country roads, his mind a jumble of memories and grief. The familiar scent of pine trees filled the air as he passed by dense woods, the late afternoon sun casting long shadows across the landscape. It had been years since he'd driven out to this lake, but today, he felt compelled to visit the spot where he and his father used to spend lazy afternoons fishing and talking about life.

The lake, nestled at the edge of Pineworth, was a hidden gem. As he parked the car and stepped out, a sense of calm washed over him. The water was still, reflecting the blue sky and the occasional cloud that drifted by. A gentle breeze rustled the leaves of the tall oaks that bordered the lake, creating a soothing rustling sound.

Sam walked to the edge of the lake, where a small wooden dock jutted out into the water. He sat down on the weathered planks, letting his feet dangle over the edge. The view from the dock hadn't changed much since his childhood. It was the same peaceful expanse of water, with cattails and lily pads dotting the shoreline. Birds chirped in the distance, and he could hear the faint sound of a boat motor somewhere across the lake.

As he sat there, Sam remembered one of those special days with his father. He must have been about ten years old, sitting on this very dock with a fishing rod in hand. His father had a quiet strength about him, and he always had a way of making Sam feel like everything was going to be okay. On that particular day, they hadn't caught much. His father had told him stories about his own childhood, about his dreams for the future, and about the importance of doing the right thing, no matter how hard it might be.

"Son," his father had said, breaking the comfortable silence, "life's like this porch. It's built to withstand storms, but sometimes the wood gets a little creaky and the paint chips. It doesn't mean you give up on it; you just keep fixing it and reinforcing it, and it stands strong again. That's what we do, you and me—we don't quit when things get tough. We find a way to make things work."

Sam remembered the feeling of the weight of those words, even though he didn't fully understand them at the time. "What if it gets too hard, Dad?" he asked, genuinely curious.

His father smiled with a gentle warmth in his eyes. "Then you find help. You call on friends, family—people who care about you. But remember, son, no matter what, never let fear guide you. Fear's like a storm: it can knock you down, but it can't keep you down if you don't let it. You get back up every time."

Now, sitting on the dock with the memory fresh in his mind, Sam felt a swell of emotion. His father's words had always been simple but powerful, and they came to him now like a beacon in the darkness. He knew that no matter how challenging the road ahead might be, he had the strength to keep going, just like his father had taught him.

Sam remembered the way his father had laughed at his jokes and shared his own wisdom in that gentle, reassuring tone. It was a simple day, but it had meant the world to Sam. Now, as he sat on the same dock, he felt a pang of loss but also a sense of gratitude for those moments they had shared.

The lake was quiet, save for the distant call of a loon. Sam closed his eyes and took a deep breath, letting the memories wash over him. He knew that his father's spirit would always be with him, guiding him as he navigated the challenges ahead. It was a bittersweet reminder that life was fleeting, but the love and lessons from those we've lost never truly faded away.

Chapter 11
Back To Duty

As Sam stepped into the familiar surroundings of the police station, a sense of purpose washed over him, driving him forward despite the heaviness in his heart. He made his way to Chief Johnson's office, ready to resume his duties and immerse himself in the distractions of work.

Chief Johnson greeted him with a somber nod, his expression mirroring the weight of the recent loss. "Sam, are you ready to return?" he asked, his tone gentle yet firm.

Sam squared his shoulders, meeting the chief's gaze with determination. "Yes, Chief," he replied without hesitation. "I'd rather be here, keeping busy, than sitting at home dwelling on things."

The chief gave him a comprehending look, his eyes reflecting a mixture of empathy and respect.

"I understand," he said quietly. "Just know that we're here for you, Sam. Take whatever time you need."

But Sam shook his head, a flicker of resolve in his eyes. "Thank you, Chief, but I need to keep moving forward," he said firmly. "My father wouldn't want me to dwell on his passing. He'd want me to focus on my duties, just like he always did."

With a solemn nod, Chief Johnson offered his support. "Very well, Sam. Take it one step at a time," he said, his voice tinged with reassurance.

"You will remain assigned to school security. If and when the protest stops you will be reassigned back on your regular shift." He continued.

As Chief Johnson delivered the news, Sam felt a surge of pride mixed with astonishment. He listened intently as the chief outlined the extension of his duties overseeing school security for another week, already mentally preparing for the challenges ahead.

But then Chief Johnson paused, and Sam's attention sharpened as the atmosphere in the room shifted. The chief's next words caught him completely off guard.

"From now on, you will be Corporal Anderson," Chief Johnson announced, his voice carrying the weight of authority and recognition. "Your performance in your assignment has been exemplary, and I believe you are deserving of this promotion."

Sam's heart skipped a beat at the unexpected declaration. The title of corporal held profound significance, signifying a new level of responsibility and leadership within the force. To hear those words spoken to him filled him with a sense of pride and accomplishment he had never felt before.

"Thank you, Chief," Sam managed to say, his voice tinged with disbelief and gratitude. "I'm honored."

Chief Johnson offered him a reassuring nod, a hint of approval in his expression. "You've earned it, Sam," he said firmly. "Now, go out there and continue to excel."

With a renewed sense of purpose, now Corporal Anderson left Chief Johnson's office, ready to embrace the challenges and responsibilities of his new rank, determined to prove himself worthy of the honor bestowed upon him.

Sam arrived at the school, the weight of his new role as Corporal settling upon his shoulders. As he entered the building, he was greeted by the familiar sight of students milling about the halls, their voices echoing off the walls.

Heading straight for the principal's office, Sam found Mr. Smith already there, poring over some paperwork. The principal looked up as Sam entered, a tired but determined expression on his face.

"Officer Anderson, good to see you," Mr. Smith greeted him, offering a weary smile. "I hope we can count on your continued support during these challenging times."

Sam returned the smile, though his thoughts were consumed by the ongoing tensions surrounding the school's integration.

"Of course, Mr. Smith," he replied, his voice laced with determination. "We're all hoping that the protests will come to an end soon."

Mr. Smith agreed. His expression reflected a mixture of concern and hope.

"We're doing everything we can to maintain order and ensure the safety of our students," the principal explained. "But it's been a difficult time for everyone involved."

Sam understood the gravity of the situation. He was acutely aware of the need for vigilance and diplomacy in the days ahead.

"We'll get through this together," Sam said with conviction, his voice steady and resolute. "I'll do whatever it takes to support you and the staff here at the school."

Mr. Smith offered a grateful nod, his eyes reflecting a glimmer of optimism amidst the uncertainty.

"Thank you, Officer Anderson," he said sincerely. "Your dedication is greatly appreciated."

Sam and his fellow officers gathered in the main lobby, preparing for the influx of students. The air was thick with anticipation, a palpable tension hanging over the building like a heavy shroud.

Sam adjusted his uniform, and his movements were methodical and precise. Beside him stood Jordan and Jamal, their expressions mirrored his own — a mixture of determination and apprehension. They exchanged brief nods of solidarity, wordlessly reaffirming their commitment to the task at hand.

The sound of footsteps echoed down the hallway as the first wave of students began to filter into the building. Sam's senses sharpened, his gaze sweeping over the crowd, searching for any signs of unrest or agitation.

As the flow of students increased, Sam and his fellow officers fell into position, strategically stationed throughout the outside of the school to ensure maximum coverage. They maintained a vigilant watch, their eyes scanning the crowd for any potential threats or disturbances.

As the morning wore on and the flow of students gradually subsided, Sam allowed himself a momentary sigh of relief. It seemed as though the protest was finally winding down, the fervor and intensity of the crowd gradually dissipating with each passing minute.

But just as Sam began to let his guard down, his attention was drawn to a familiar figure emerging from across the parking lot. It was the same man he had seen earlier in the day, the one who had instigated trouble with the family at the school entrance.

A surge of apprehension coursed through Sam's veins as he watched the man's approach. His instincts told him trouble was brewing, the tension in the air thickening with each step the man took.

Sam exchanged a brief glance with Jordan and Jamal, silently communicating the urgency of the situation. They fell into step beside him, their movements purposeful and determined as they closed the distance between themselves and the approaching figure.

As the man drew nearer, Sam could see the steely determination etched into his features, the simmering anger barely contained beneath the surface. It was clear that he was not here to peacefully protest – he was here for something else entirely.

Sam's heart quickened with apprehension as he braced himself for whatever confrontation lay ahead. He knew that he and his fellow officers would need to act swiftly and decisively to defuse the situation before it escalated into something far more dangerous.

As the officers advanced towards the man, a car suddenly veered into the parking lot, its tires screeching against the asphalt. It seemed oblivious to the unfolding tension, as if it were just another mundane morning drop-off.

Sam's instincts screamed danger, but there was no time to react. The car wedged itself between them and the man, blocking their line of sight. Sam's heart hammered in his chest as he watched, a knot of dread forming in the pit of his stomach.

The occupants of the car seemed oblivious to the charged atmosphere around them, absorbed in their own world.

Time seemed to slow to a crawl as the scene unfolded before Sam's eyes. The air crackled with tension, each heartbeat echoing loudly in his ears as he watched the car pull into the space between them and the man.

His gaze fixated on the figure stepping out of the car – a young black woman, her presence a stark contrast to the simmering hostility that hung heavy in the air. She waved goodbye to her mother, oblivious to the danger lurking just yards away.

But before Sam could react, before he could even comprehend what was happening, the man's voice sliced through the silence like a blade. "You don't belong here," he bellowed, his words dripping with venomous hatred.

In an instant, the peaceful morning shattered into chaos. The man's hand darted into the depths of his jacket, emerging with something clenched tightly in his fist. Sam's heart lurched in his chest as he braced himself for the worst, his mind racing with a million different scenarios, each more terrifying than the last.

With adrenaline coursing through his veins, Sam's training kicked in. "Get down!" he bellowed, lunging towards the young girl with desperate urgency. His outstretched arm collided with her, knocking her off her feet and sending her sprawling to the ground.

The deafening crack of gunfire shattered the air, echoing through the stillness of the morning. Sam's heart skipped a beat as he shielded the girl with his own body, bracing for impact. Several more shots rang out in quick succession, each one a chilling reminder of the danger lurking nearby.

As the echoes faded into eerie silence, Sam dared to steal a glance at the girl beneath him. Her wide eyes reflected a mix of shock and fear, her breaths coming in ragged gasps. Relief flooded through him as he saw that she was unharmed, but the ordeal had left its mark on her, etched into the lines of her trembling frame.

"Are you okay?" Sam asked, his voice soft and concerned.

Sam's breath caught as the girl's voice cut through the chaos, pulling him back to the present moment. "Sir?" she uttered, her concern palpable as she took in the scene unfolding before her. "You are hurt."

Sam's gaze flickered down to his right shoulder, where a dull ache throbbed in tandem with his pounding heart. Blood seeped through his uniform, staining the fabric a dark crimson, but the shock of the injury had dulled the pain for now.

"Don't worry," he reassured her, his voice strained but steady. "I'll be okay." Despite the adrenaline coursing through his veins, a sense of urgency gnawed at him, urging him to stay focused, to keep moving forward.

The scene was fraught with tension, every nerve in Sam's body taut with anticipation. As he turned, his eyes widened, taking in the chaotic tableau before him. The acrid scent of burnt gunpowder lingered in the air, mingling with the metallic tang of blood. Sirens wailed in the distance, their mournful cries echoing through the tumultuous scene.

Amidst the chaos, the sharp crack of gunfire reverberated, followed by the frantic shouts of officers, their voices a discordant symphony of urgency. Sam's heart hammered in his chest, the rhythmic thud drowning out all other sounds as he raced to assess the situation.

His eyes fell upon Jordan and Jamal, their figures silhouetted against the backdrop of the sprawling schoolyard. Their faces were etched with determination, their movements swift and purposeful as they tended to the fallen man. Sam could sense the tension in the air, thick and palpable, like a heavy blanket weighing down on his shoulders.

The scene unfolded in a blur of motion and noise, the frantic energy of the moment electrifying the air. Emergency lights flashed, casting eerie shadows across the pavement as officers rushed to secure the area. The distant wail of approaching sirens grew louder, a harbinger of hope amidst the chaos.

As Chief Johnson arrived on the scene, the chaos of the moment seemed to subside, replaced by a sense of urgency and authority. He made his way through the crowd, his presence commanding attention amidst the commotion.

Approaching Sam, who stood amidst the flurry of activity with a stoic resolve, Chief Johnson wasted no time in assessing the situation. With practiced efficiency, he guided the ambulance through the throngs of officers and onlookers, ensuring that it reached Sam's side without delay.

But Sam, ever the picture of resilience, brushed off Chief Johnson's concern with a shake of his head. "I'm fine, Chief," he insisted, his voice steady despite the adrenaline coursing through his veins. "Just a scratch."

But Chief Johnson was having none of it. With a firmness born of years of experience, he delivered his command with unwavering authority. "That's an order, Anderson," he said, his tone leaving no room for argument. "Get in the ambulance. Your duty is done for today."

As the ambulance doors swung open, Sam knew that he had no choice but to comply. With one last glance at the scene unfolding around him, he climbed into the back of the ambulance, the weight of the day's events settling heavily on his shoulders.

As the door of the ambulance began to swing shut, Jordan dashed forward, his footsteps echoing against the pavement as he closed the distance between them in swift strides.

Breathless but determined, he reached Sam just in time, his voice urgent yet filled with a deep sense of camaraderie.

"Sam, I'll be there at the hospital later, alright? You did a great job today," Jordan exclaimed, a testament to the respect and admiration he held for his fellow officer. With a reassuring pat on Sam's good shoulder, he added, "I'll let your mom know you're on your way there."

Concern etched into his features, Sam turned to Jordan with a question heavy on his lips. "Did... did he make it?" he asked, his voice barely above a whisper, the weight of the day's events hanging heavily in the air between them.

Jordan's response was a solemn shake of the head, a silent acknowledgment of the tragedy that had unfolded before them.

As the ambulance raced toward the hospital, the chaos of the day began to fade, replaced by the throbbing ache in Sam's shoulder. With each bump in the road, the pain intensified, a stark reminder of the events that had unfolded just moments before.

Despite the discomfort, a sense of relief washed over Sam. He couldn't shake the feeling of satisfaction knowing that he had saved the girl's life, that his quick actions had prevented a tragedy. And yet, there was a somber recognition that their assailant had been stopped by more drastic means—a sobering reminder of the harsh realities of their line of work.

The presence of Jordan and Jamal provided a sense of reassurance amidst the chaos. Their swift response and unwavering support had been instrumental in containing the situation. Sam felt a surge of gratitude toward his fellow officers, knowing that they had his back when he needed them most.

As he recalled the frantic moments leading up to the confrontation, Sam couldn't help but feel a sense of pride in their collective response. Jordan's steady presence and Jamal's quick thinking had complimented his own actions, creating a seamless effort to protect the innocent.

With a silent nod of appreciation, Sam acknowledged the bond that united them, forged through countless shared experiences and the unwavering commitment to their duty. Together, they formed a formidable team—a force for good in a world fraught with uncertainty. As the ambulance raced toward the hospital, Sam found solace in the knowledge that he wasn't alone in facing the challenges that lay ahead.

Deep in thought, Sam reflected on the complexities of the situation. He had never wished for someone's death, but he understood that sometimes, in the heat of the moment, it was the only way to prevent further harm. It was a bitter truth, one that weighed heavily on his conscience even as the ambulance sped toward the hospital, its siren wailing in the distance.

Sam's heart skipped a beat as he caught sight of Natalie's familiar face amidst the flurry of activity outside the hospital. Despite the worry etched on her features, her presence brought him a sense of comfort and relief.

As Natalie rushed toward him, her concern palpable in every step, Sam felt a surge of gratitude wash over him. Her genuine care and unwavering support were a beacon of light in the midst of his turmoil. "I'm okay," he assured her, his voice laced with gratitude and reassurance.

Natalie's eyes searched his face, her concern refusing to wane as she reached out to touch his arm gently. "You scared me," she admitted softly, her words echoing the depth of her worry.

With a half-hearted grin, Sam attempted to lighten the mood. "Guess I should consider myself lucky to have a nurse waiting for me. Who knows, maybe I'll start inventing reasons to come by more often," he quipped, though his attempt at humor was tempered by the gravity of the situation.

Natalie's lips curved into a faint smile at Sam's attempt at humor, though the worry still lingered in her eyes. "You know I'm always here for you, whether you're in need of medical attention or not," she replied with a gentle, teasing tone, her words infused with warmth and affection.

Sam chuckled softly, the tension in his shoulders easing slightly at her familiar banter. "Well, I'll try not to make it a habit of getting injured just to see you," he quipped, his tone light despite the seriousness of the situation.

Their exchange brought a brief moment of levity amidst the gravity of the day's events, a reminder of the bond they shared and the comfort of having someone to lean on in times of need.

Chapter 12
The Process Of Healing

AS SAM LAY IN HIS HOSPITAL bed, the soft light filtering through the curtains cast a gentle glow over the room. The rhythmic beeping of the heart monitor provided a steady backdrop to the quiet hum of activity in the hallway beyond.

His mind was still reeling from the events of the day—the chaos, the fear, and the sudden rush of adrenaline that had propelled him into action. But now, as he lay there in the relative calm of the hospital room, he couldn't help but feel a sense of relief wash over him.

The door creaked open, and his mother hurried in, her steps quick with worry. "Sam, oh Sam," she exclaimed, her voice thick with emotion as she rushed to his side. "Are you alright? What happened?"

Sam offered her a reassuring smile, reaching out to take her hand in his. "I'm okay, Mom," he assured her, his voice steady despite the lingering echoes of adrenaline in his veins. "It's not as bad as it looks."

Shortly after, the doctor entered, his white coat crisp against the sterile backdrop of the hospital room. With a calm demeanor, he informed Sam of the relatively minor nature of his injury. "The bullet went clean through," he explained, his voice a reassuring presence amidst the turmoil.

"As long as you keep the wound clean and follow our instructions, it shouldn't pose any long-term issues."

As Sam's mom exited the room with a reassuring smile, Jordan stepped inside, his presence bringing a sense of familiarity and comfort to the hospital room. Sam watched as his mother disappeared down the hallway, leaving him alone with his friend.

"Hey, Sam," Jordan said softly, his voice filled with concern as he approached the side of the bed. "How are you holding up?"

Sam managed a weak smile, grateful for Jordan's presence. "Hey, Jordan," he replied, his voice hoarse from the strain of the day's events. "I've been better, but I'll live."

"You had us worried there for a minute."

Sam offered him a weak smile. "Sorry about that," he replied, his voice still raspy from the adrenaline. "Things got a little crazy back there."

Jordan's eyes flickered with understanding. "Yeah, they sure did," he agreed, his gaze drifting to the window for a moment before returning to Sam. "Listen, I wanted to thank you for what you did out there. You saved that girl's life."

Sam shook his head, his expression solemn. "I just did what I had to do," he said quietly, his thoughts drifting back to the chaotic moments outside the school. "I'm just glad everyone's okay."

"I wasn't even sure what was happening after I knocked the girl down," he continued.

"We exchanged fire," Jordan confirmed, his voice low and serious. "Jamal and I had to take action to protect you and the others."

Sam's mind was still reeling from the chaos of the moment. "I appreciate it, Jordan," he murmured, his voice tinged with exhaustion. "I honestly don't remember much after I pushed the girl down."

Jordan placed a reassuring hand on Sam's arm, offering him a supportive squeeze. "It's okay, Sam," he said gently. "You did what you had to do to keep her safe. That's what matters."

Sam offered him a faint smile, grateful for Jordan's understanding. "Thanks, man," he replied, his voice filled with gratitude. "I don't know, part of me was afraid. Afraid that maybe I made the wrong decision."

Jordan placed a reassuring hand on Sam's shoulder. "It's natural to feel afraid in a situation like that, Sam. But it's what you do in that moment that defines you."

Sam absorbed Jordan's wisdom. "I just knew I had to do something. I couldn't stand by and let that girl get hurt."

"And that's exactly what you did," Jordan affirmed. "You made a decision, and you stuck with it. That takes courage, Sam. Real courage."

Sam let out a sigh, feeling a weight lift off his shoulders. "Thanks, Jordan. I appreciate that."

Jordan smiled. "Anytime, Sam. Just remember, fear is just a feeling. It's what you do with it that matters."

Jordan continued, his expression reflecting their shared sense of camaraderie. "We've always got each other's backs," he said firmly.

As they sat together in the quiet hospital room, the weight of the day's events hanging heavy in the air, Sam felt a sense of reassurance,e knowing that Jordan was there beside him.

As the evening sun cast its golden rays through the hospital window, Sam's thoughts turned to the familiar comforts of home. He had spent hours under the watchful care of the hospital staff; his mind occupied with thoughts of the day's events and the uncertain road that lay ahead. But now, as the doctor pronounced him fit for discharge, a sense of relief washed over him.

With his belongings gathered and his discharge papers in hand, Sam prepared to leave the sterile confines of the hospital behind. As he made his way through the corridors, his steps buoyed by the prospect of returning home, he couldn't shake the feeling of gratitude for the support he had received during his time here.

His mother was waiting for him at the hospital entrance, her eyes bright with concern and love. Beside her stood Natalie, a steadfast presence by his side throughout his ordeal. As Sam approached, his mother greeted him with a warm embrace, her relief palpable as she welcomed him back into her arms.

Turning to Natalie, his mother offered a heartfelt invitation. "Why don't you come over, dear?" she suggested, her voice filled with kindness. "You've been such a comfort to us during this difficult time. It would mean the world to me to have you join us for dinner."

Natalie's eyes sparkled with gratitude as she accepted the invitation.

As Sam sat in his father's old rocking chair, feeling the weight of the day's events settle around him, he found solace in the comforting presence of Natalie and his mother. From the moment she arrived, Natalie had seamlessly integrated herself into their home, offering her support and companionship in their time of need.

Listening to the gentle cadence of their voices as they conversed, Sam couldn't help but marvel at the easy rapport between them. Despite only meeting on two occasions – first at his father's death and now during his recovery – Natalie and his mother seemed to share an instant connection, their laughter mingling with shared memories and heartfelt conversation.

As he watched them from his seat by the window, bathed in the soft glow of the evening light, Sam felt a profound sense of gratitude wash over him. In the midst of loss and uncertainty, he found comfort in the bond that had formed between these two important women in his life. They may have come together under challenging circumstances, but in that moment, they were united by a shared sense of compassion, understanding, and resilience.

As they settled into the cozy living room of Sam's childhood home, his mother couldn't resist the opportunity to share a bit of lighthearted teasing. With a mischievous twinkle in her eye, she reached for the dusty photo album tucked away on the nearby bookshelf.

"Let's take a trip down memory lane, shall we?" his mother exclaimed with a playful grin, flipping through the pages until she found what she was looking for. "Ah, here we go!"

Before Sam could protest, his mother proudly displayed a series of adorable baby photos, each one capturing a chubby-cheeked infant sporting an array of comical expressions. As she eagerly narrated each snapshot, recounting tales of Sam's early adventures and misadventures, Sam couldn't help but feel a mixture of embarrassment and amusement.

"Oh, come on, Mom," Sam protested good-naturedly, his cheeks flushing with embarrassment as Natalie stifled a giggle beside him. "Do you have to show her all of those?"

But his mother was undeterred, her laughter filling the room as she regaled Natalie with tales of Sam's antics as a chubby-cheeked infant. "You were such a chunky little baby," she teased, her eyes twinkling with affection. "But oh, so adorable!"

Natalie joined in the laughter, her easy going demeanor putting Sam at ease as she joked along with his mother. "Well, at least you've grown into those cheeks," she quipped, her playful banter earning her a playful swat from Sam.

As they enjoyed the pleasant chatter and shared laughter, Sam's mother's curiosity was piqued. With a warm smile, she turned her attention to Natalie and inquired, "So, how did you two become friends?"

Natalie's eyes sparkled with fond reminiscence as she leaned back comfortably in her chair, her expression thoughtful as she recalled the chance encounter that had brought her into Sam's life.

"It was actually quite serendipitous," Natalie began, her voice soft with nostalgia. "I was at the cemetery in town one afternoon, enjoying the sunshine and taking a leisurely stroll with my sister Nadia, when we happened to stumble upon Sam here."

Sam's mother listened attentively. Her interest was piqued as Natalie continued to weave her tale.

"We struck up a conversation, and before we knew it, we were chatting away like old friends,"

Natalie explained, her smile growing wider with each passing moment. "There was just something about Sam's easygoing nature and genuine warmth that drew me in."

Sam's mother showed her understanding, her eyes twinkling with affection as she glanced fondly at her son. "He has always had a way of making friends wherever he goes," she remarked proudly.

Natalie agreed, her gaze softening as she turned back to Sam. "Indeed he does," she replied, her voice filled with warmth and admiration. "And I feel lucky to count myself among them."

As Natalie prepared to leave, Sam and his mother walked her to the door, their expressions filled with gratitude for her visit. Sam's mother offered heartfelt thanks for Natalie's company and concern, expressing how much she appreciated her kindness during a difficult time.

"It was wonderful to see you again, Natalie," Sam chimed in, a genuine smile gracing his lips.

"Thanks for coming by."

Natalie returned their warm sentiments with a smile of her own, her eyes reflecting a genuine sense of care and camaraderie. "Of course, anytime," she replied softly. "Take care, both of you."

With a final wave and a parting smile, Natalie stepped out into the evening.

As they settled back into their seats after Natalie's departure, Sam's mother turned to him, her gaze filled with curiosity and warmth. "So, Sam," she began, "how close are you and Natalie?"

Sam paused for a moment, considering his response. "Well, Mom," he replied with a thoughtful smile, "we've gotten to be really good friends, I'd say."

His mother appeared happy, a knowing smile playing at the corners of her lips. "That's lovely to hear," she remarked, her voice tinged with a hint of affection. "She seems like a wonderful person."

"Yeah, she is," Sam agreed, a genuine fondness evident in his tone. "I'm grateful to have her as a friend."

Sam's mother's words carried a weight of concern and caution, her tone gentle yet tinged with underlying worry. "Sam," she began, her voice soft but earnest, "I like Natalie, I really do. But you know how things are around here, especially with race relations. I just want you to be careful, okay? I'm not saying you shouldn't hang out with her or anything like that, but just... be careful."

Sam listened to his mother's words, her concern resonating with him deeply. He acknowledged the validity of her advice. "I hear you, Mom," he replied, his voice reflecting a mix of reassurance and gratitude. "I'll be careful, I promise. Natalie's a good friend, and I'll make sure to look out for both of us."

His mother offered him a small smile, her eyes conveying a blend of maternal love and a lingering sense of worry. "Thank you, Sam," she said softly, her hand reaching out to gently squeeze his shoulder. "I trust you to make the right decisions. Just remember to stay safe out there, okay?"

Sam returned his mother's smile, a sense of determination shining in his eyes. "I will, Mom," he affirmed, a newfound sense of responsibility settling within him. "I'll make sure of it."

Chapter 13
A Town In Healing

AS SAM FOCUSED ON RECUPERATING from his injury, the town of Pineworth was also undergoing a process of healing in the aftermath of the incident. The news of the altercation had spread far and wide, reaching national headlines and sparking conversations across the country. In the midst of this attention, Mayor Carter emerged as a voice of unity and reassurance for the community.

Mayor Carter's public appearance was a pivotal moment as he stood before the gathered crowd and addressed the events that had unfolded. With a firm yet empathetic tone, he emphasized the fundamental principle that the Pineworth Police Department was dedicated to protecting every citizen, regardless of race or background.

His words carried weight, echoing through the streets of Pineworth and resonating with residents who had been shaken by recent events. The mayor's commitment to justice and equality instilled a sense of confidence and unity in the town's collective consciousness.

As Sam followed the developments from his home, he felt a surge of pride for his town and its leadership. The journey toward healing was far from over, but Mayor Carter's message marked a crucial step forward.

As Sam sat on his front porch, soaking in the gentle breeze of the late afternoon, his attention was drawn to the sound of a car pulling into his driveway. Squinting against the sunlight, he recognized Jimmy Winters' familiar pickup truck, with his son Henry riding shotgun.

"Hey there, Sam!" Jimmy greeted warmly as he stepped out of the vehicle, his easy smile reaching his eyes.

"Hey, Jimmy. Henry," Sam replied, returning the greeting.

Henry, a young man with a friendly demeanor, offered a nod in response.

Jimmy chuckled as he approached. "Henry here insisted we swing by and check on you. Said he wanted to see that bullet hole for himself."

Sam laughed, shaking his head. "Well, I hate to disappoint, but I'm not exactly keen on showing off battle scars."

Henry grinned sheepishly. "Can't blame a guy for being curious, right?"

"Of course not," Sam replied with a chuckle. "But I'm doing alright, all things considered. Thanks for stopping by, both of you."

Jimmy paused for a moment, his expression turning more earnest as he looked at Sam. "You know, Sam, your grandfather, and your father would be mighty proud of the man you've become. Standing up for what's right, serving your community... that's the Anderson way."

Sam felt a lump form in his throat at Jimmy's words. Coming from a man who had known his family for generations, it carried a weight that touched him deeply. "Thank you, Jimmy. That means a lot, coming from you."

Jimmy gave a somber yet comforting smile on his face. "You keep your head held high, Sam. You're doing good work out there. Your family's legacy is in good hands."

With a firm handshake and a parting nod, Jimmy and Henry made their way back to the truck, leaving Sam to ponder the significance of their brief but heartfelt exchange.

Sam took the newspaper with a mixture of surprise and gratitude, his eyes scanning the bold headline. "Local police save girl's life," it read in large, prominent letters. It was surreal to see his name and the events of that tumultuous day splashed across the front page.

"Thanks," Sam said to the mailman, offering a nod of appreciation. "Guess I made the front page, huh?"

The mailman chuckled, nodding. "Sure did, sir. Quite the hero, if you ask me."

Sam offered a modest smile, feeling a sense of pride mixed with humility. Being recognized for his actions felt strange yet validating. As the mailman drove off, Sam settled into his porch chair, the newspaper in hand, contemplating the gravity of what had transpired and the newfound attention it had brought him.

His mother stepped outside, her expression one of gentle concern as she approached him, carrying a tray with two glasses of lemonade.

"Hey, sweetheart," she greeted, her voice soft and comforting. "How are you feeling?"

Sam managed a small smile as he accepted one of the glasses from her, the cool condensation soothing against his fingers. "Better, Mom. Thanks," he replied, taking a sip of the refreshing drink.

His mother settled into the chair beside him, her gaze turning thoughtful as she set her glass down on the table between them.

"You know, Chief Johnson called earlier to check in on you," she began, her tone gentle. "He mentioned that the girl you saved and her family want to meet you. They just want to say thank you."

Sam's brows furrowed in surprise, his mind racing at the thought of meeting the family whose lives he had touched. "Really?" he asked, a mix of uncertainty and curiosity in his voice. "I mean, yeah, I'd like to meet them, but... I don't know if I'm ready for that yet."

His mother reached out and rested her hand reassuringly on his shoulder. "Take your time, Sam. It's a lot to process, I know. But they just want to express their gratitude, that's all."

Sam offered a small, grateful smile, appreciating his mother's understanding. "Yeah, I'll think about it. Thanks, Mom."

As they sat in companionable silence, the gentle rustle of leaves in the breeze providing a soothing backdrop, Sam couldn't help but feel a sense of gratitude for the support of his family in such trying times.

"Hey, Mom," Sam called out gently as he put the newspaper down, his expression soft yet resolute. "I think I'm gonna take a walk over to the cemetery for a bit. Just need some time to clear my head, you know?"

His mother turned to face him, concern etched into her features. "Are you sure, sweetheart? It's getting late, and you're still recovering," she replied, her voice tinged with maternal worry.

Sam offered her a reassuring smile, the glint of determination in his eyes reflecting his resolve.

"Yeah, Mom, I'll be fine. Besides, I could use the fresh air," he reassured her, reaching out to squeeze her hand gently.

As Sam's mother watched him rise from his chair, a mixture of concern and pride reflected in her eyes. She knew her son's resilience, but she also understood the toll recent events had taken on him.

"Alright, sweetheart," she said, her voice gentle yet supportive. "Just be careful out there, okay?"

Sam offered her a reassuring smile, his gratitude evident in his eyes as he placed a hand on her shoulder. "I will, Mom. Thanks," he replied, the warmth of their bond palpable in the air.

With a nod of farewell, Sam made his way down the steps of the porch and onto the sidewalk, the familiar path to the cemetery beckoning him with a sense of quiet solace. Despite the ache in his shoulder and the weight of recent events still heavy on his mind, he found comfort in the thought of visiting his father's grave, a place of grounding and reflection amidst the chaos of the world around him.

As he walked, the gentle breeze whispered through the trees, the sound a soothing accompaniment to his thoughts. With each step, Sam felt a sense of peace settle over him, a reminder that even in the midst of adversity, there were moments of tranquility to be found.

Arriving at the entrance to the cemetery, Sam paused, his gaze sweeping over the rows of headstones with a mixture of reverence and nostalgia. He made his way to his father's resting place, the familiar marker a silent reminder of the man who had shaped his life in so many ways.

Standing before the grave, Sam took a moment to reflect, the memories of his father flooding his mind with a bittersweet intensity. He spoke softly to the silent stone, sharing his thoughts and feelings with the one person who had always been there for him, even in death.

"Hey, Dad," he began softly, his voice carrying a mixture of emotion and determination. "I wish you were here to see everything that's been happening lately. You always said I'd make something of myself, and I hope I'm living up to that."

He paused, collecting his thoughts before continuing. "You'd be proud, Dad. I saved someone's life the other day," he said, a hint of awe in his voice as he recounted the events of the shooting. "It was intense, Dad. I didn't know if I was gonna make it out of there, but I did. And I'm here now, talking to you."

A gentle breeze rustled through the trees, the sound a soothing backdrop to his words. "I miss you, Dad. Every day. But I know you're watching over me, guiding me through all of this," he said, his voice filled with a quiet resolve.

"I'll keep doing my best, Dad. For you, for Mom, for everyone," he vowed, his words a silent promise echoing in the stillness of the cemetery.

After a time, Sam felt a sense of closure wash over him, a renewed strength and determination rising within his heart. With a final glance at his father's grave, he turned and began to walk once more, the quiet beauty of the cemetery offering him a sense of peace and clarity that he carried with him as he made his way back home.

Sam spotted Jamal as he made his way out of the cemetery, his presence a welcome sight amidst the somber surroundings. He approached Jamal with a nod of acknowledgment, a silent understanding passing between them.

"Hey, Jamal," Sam greeted, his voice carrying a sense of camaraderie. "How's it going?"

Jamal's concern was palpable as he glanced at Sam's injured shoulder. "Glad to see you're still standing," he remarked, his words carrying a sense of solidarity.

Sam nodded in acknowledgment, grateful for Jamal's support. "Thanks, man," he replied sincerely. "It's been a rough ride, but I'll get through it."

"So, how are things now that you're on your own?" Sam continued.

Jamal returned the smile, though there was a hint of exhaustion in his eyes. "I'm doing alright," he replied, his tone carrying a mix of sincerity and reflection. "It's been a bit different now that I'm not glued to Jordan's side anymore."

Sam recalled his own days as a rookie officer. "I can imagine," he remarked. "Must feel liberating in a way, not being a rookie anymore."

Jamal's expression brightened at the observation. "Yeah, it's definitely been a change," he admitted, a note of pride creeping into his voice. "I'm starting to find my footing, you know? Learning to trust my instincts more."

Sam was glad to hear Jamal's sense of confidence growing. "That's great to hear," he remarked. "You've come a long way since you first joined the force."

Jamal chuckled modestly, his gaze drifting to the peaceful surroundings of the town square. "Thanks, Sam. Means a lot coming from you," he replied, genuine appreciation coloring his words. "It's been a journey, that's for sure."

"Jamal," Sam began, his tone earnest as he turned to face the younger officer. "I want to share something with you, something I've come to realize during my time on the force."

Jamal listened intently, his attention fully focused on Sam's words.

"This job," Sam continued, his voice carrying a weight of conviction, "is more than just enforcing laws or responding to calls. It's about making a difference in people's lives, even when it feels like the odds are stacked against us."

Jamal shook his head up and down, understanding the gravity of Sam's message.

"We're entrusted with a responsibility, Jamal," Sam went on, his gaze reflecting the sincerity of his words. "To protect and serve, yes, but also to be a source of hope and reassurance for our community. Especially in times of uncertainty or fear."

As Sam spoke, Jamal could sense the depth of experience and wisdom behind his words, a testament to the journey Sam had traveled as an officer.

"We may not always have all the answers, Jamal," Sam acknowledged, a hint of humility in his voice, "but as long as we approach each day with integrity, compassion, and a commitment to doing what's right, we can make a difference, no matter how small it may seem."

Jamal absorbed Sam's words, feeling a newfound sense of purpose and determination stirring within him.

"Hey, Jamal, I know Jordan was joking earlier, but I want you to know something. I see something special in you."

Jamal looked at Sam, surprise flickering in his eyes. "Really? What do you mean?"

"You've got the 'it' factor, Jamal," Sam continued, his tone unwavering. "You're smart, you're capable, and you've got compassion. That's something you can't teach."

A hint of disbelief crossed Jamal's face, but Sam's earnestness was undeniable. "Thanks, Sam. I appreciate that. Coming from you, it means a lot."

Sam felt a sense of pride swelling within him. "Just keep doing what you're doing, Jamal. You've got a bright future ahead of you in this profession."

"Thanks, Sam," Jamal said, gratitude evident in his voice. "I'll keep all that in mind as I continue on this journey."

A sense of satisfaction washed over him. At that moment, he knew that he had passed on more than just advice to Jamal—he had shared a piece of his own dedication and belief in the importance of their work.

As Sam bid farewell to Jamal, he felt a sense of camaraderie and shared purpose that buoyed his spirits. Watching Jamal walk away, he couldn't help but feel a twinge of pride, knowing that he had played a small part in guiding the younger officer.

Taking a deep breath, Sam began to stroll through the town square, his gaze sweeping over the familiar sights and sounds of Pineworth. There was a palpable shift in the atmosphere—a subtle yet unmistakable sense of unity and resolve that seemed to linger in the air.

The community, it appeared, was ready to move forward, eager to leave the tumultuous events surrounding the school integration behind them. As Sam passed by the bustling shops and bustling streets, he couldn't help but feel a swell of optimism wash over him.

It was a hopeful sign, a testament to the resilience and strength of the people of Pineworth. Despite the challenges they had faced, they were determined to come together, to rebuild and renew their sense of community.

And for Sam, it was a reassuring reminder that even in the face of adversity, there was always hope. Hope for a brighter future, for a better tomorrow—a tomorrow that he knew, with unwavering certainty, they would build together, one step at a time.

Chapter 14
A New Beginning

AS SAM AWOKE ON THE morning of his return to work, he felt a mixture of anticipation and apprehension coursing through him. It had been weeks since he had last donned his uniform, weeks filled with recovery, reflection, and a mounting sense of restlessness. Now, as he prepared to re-enter the familiar rhythm of his duties, he couldn't shake the lingering doubts that nagged at the edges of his mind.

With a sigh, Sam swung his legs out of bed and made his way to his dresser, where his uniform lay neatly folded. Running his fingers over the familiar fabric, he couldn't help but feel a surge of nostalgia for the sense of purpose it represented. But alongside that nostalgia lingered a hint of trepidation—a gnawing uncertainty about what awaited him beyond the confines of his home.

As he dressed, the weight of his injury pressed heavily on his mind, a constant reminder of the dangers inherent in his line of work. Yet beneath the surface of his apprehension, there lay a stubborn resolve, a quiet determination to face whatever challenges lay ahead with courage and conviction.

With a final adjustment to his uniform, Sam stood before the mirror, his reflection a portrait of stoic determination. Stepping out into the morning light, he felt a sense of renewal wash over him, a renewed sense of purpose that buoyed his spirits and steeled his resolve for the day ahead.

As Sam slid behind the wheel of his patrol car, the familiar scent of leather and polished metal enveloped him, mingling with the crisp morning air that seeped through the open window. The engine purred to life with a reassuring hum, a sound that was as familiar to him as his own heartbeat.

With practiced ease, Sam navigated the winding streets of Pineworth, each turn and curve etched into his memory like the lines of an old friend's face. The quiet hum of the engine provided a steady backdrop to his thoughts as he made his way towards the police station, the rhythmic thump of tires against pavement echoing the steady cadence of his heartbeat.

The streets were still and serene in the early morning light, bathed in the soft glow of dawn's first light. Sam's gaze drifted to familiar landmarks that dotted the landscape, each one a silent sentinel that stood witness to the ebb and flow of life in the small town.

As he drove, memories flickered through his mind like snippets of an old film reel, each one a snapshot of moments long past. He passed the corner where he and his friends used to gather after school, the park where he had shared his first kiss, and the diner where he and his father used to go for breakfast on Saturday mornings.

With each passing mile, the weight of his recent experiences began to lift, replaced by a sense of purpose and resolve. The road ahead stretched out before him, a blank canvas waiting to be painted with new memories and experiences. And as the station loomed into view, Sam couldn't help but feel a surge of anticipation for the challenges and adventures that lay ahead.

As Sam entered the bustling briefing room, the sight that greeted him caught him off guard. Applause erupted from his fellow officers, their faces a mix of admiration and relief. Sam felt a swell of gratitude wash over him at the warm welcome, but beneath the surface, a wave of discomfort rippled through him.

He appreciated the gesture; he truly did, but the spotlight felt uncomfortable, almost suffocating. Sam had never been one to seek out attention or accolades; he preferred to let his actions speak for themselves. And now, as the focus of everyone's gaze, he couldn't help but feel a pang of self-consciousness.

As the applause died down and the room settled into a hushed silence, Sam offered a nod of acknowledgment, his expression a blend of humility and gratitude. He was grateful for the support of his colleagues, grateful for their unwavering solidarity in the face of adversity. But even as he took his seat among them, a part of him longed for the quiet anonymity of his routine duties, away from the spotlight and the scrutiny of those around him.

As the briefing came to an end, Chief Johnson called Sam over. "Sam, I need you to head over to the high school."

"Sir, may I ask why I'm needed at the school?" Sam inquired, his brow furrowing with curiosity as he approached Chief Johnson.

The chief glanced up from his desk, his expression unreadable for a moment before he responded. "Cpl Anderson, this talent show should be of interest to you," he replied cryptically, his tone giving nothing away.

Sam's confusion deepened at the chief's enigmatic words, but he agreed nonetheless. "Yes sir," he said, his voice steady despite the uncertainty swirling within him. He trusted Chief Johnson's judgment, even if he didn't fully understand the reasoning behind the assignment.

Sam made his way out of the briefing room and towards the exit, his mind buzzing with questions and possibilities. As he climbed into his patrol car and set off toward the school, he couldn't shake the feeling that there was more to this assignment than met the eye.

As Sam stepped into the familiar halls of the high school, he was met by Principal Smith, who greeted him with a warm smile. "Cpl. Anderson, it's good to see you," the principal said, extending his hand in gratitude. "Thank you for your swift action that day. You made a real difference."

Sam smiled, accepting the principal's handshake with a sense of humility. "It's all part of the job, Principal Smith," he replied, his voice carrying a quiet strength. "I'm just glad I could help."

Principal Smith expressed appreciatively before guiding Sam through the bustling corridors towards the gymnasium, their footsteps echoing against the tiled floor.

"We've got something special planned for the students today," the principal explained, his tone filled with anticipation. "I think you'll enjoy it."

As they reached the gym, Mr. Smith held open the door, gesturing for Sam to enter. "Welcome to the talent show, Officer Anderson," he said with a smile, his eyes twinkling with excitement. "I hope you'll find it entertaining."

Sam offered a grateful nod as he stepped into the gym, taking in the lively atmosphere and the buzz of excitement from the students gathered inside. It was a stark contrast to the tension he had felt during his previous visits, and he couldn't help but feel a sense of relief wash over him.

Finding a seat near the front, Sam settled in, his gaze sweeping over the colorful decorations and the eager faces of the audience. Despite the challenges they had faced, there was a palpable sense of unity and resilience in the air—a testament to the strength of the community.

Sam found himself immersed in the excitement of the talent show. As each student took the stage to showcase their skills, he couldn't help but be captivated by the diverse talents on display.

From heartfelt musical performances to awe-inspiring dance routines, the students poured their hearts into their performances, each one leaving a lasting impression on Sam. As the event went on, he found himself cheering alongside the audience, swept up in the energy and enthusiasm of the moment.

Yet, amidst the laughter and applause, a question lingered in the back of Sam's mind: why was he here? Despite the enjoyable distraction, he couldn't shake the feeling that there was more to his presence at the talent show than met the eye.

Nevertheless, Sam pushed aside his doubts for the time being, choosing instead to focus on the joy of the event. After all, he reasoned, sometimes the answers we seek reveal themselves in the most unexpected of places.

As Mr Smith announced the final act of the evening, Sam's attention sharpened. His heart skipped a beat as he watched a familiar figure step onto the stage. It was the same girl he had shielded from harm during the chaotic incident outside the school.

A surge of emotions washed over Sam as he watched her take her place under the spotlight. Memories of that harrowing day flooded back, the sound of gunfire echoing in his mind. Yet, here she was, standing tall and confident in front of the crowd, ready to share her talent with the world.

Sam's gaze remained fixed on her, his heart swelling with pride and admiration. Despite the adversity she had faced, she refused to be defined by fear or uncertainty. Instead, she embraced the opportunity to shine, showcasing her resilience and determination for all to see.

"Ladies and gentlemen," Mr. Smith's voice boomed over the microphone, drawing everyone's attention to the stage. "It is with great pleasure that I introduce our next performer, a remarkable young lady whose talent knows no bounds. Please give a warm welcome to Emily Davis!"

The crowd erupted into applause as Emily stepped forward, a confident smile gracing her lips. Her presence commanded the stage as Mr. Smith continued to sing her praises. "Emily will be sharing with us a piece of her own creation—a powerful poem that speaks to the strength and resilience we all possess."

As Emily took a deep breath and prepared to begin, Sam felt a surge of anticipation ripple through him. He had seen her bravery in the face of danger, and now he was about to witness her artistic prowess firsthand.

As the room hushed in anticipation, Emily stepped onto the stage, her presence commanding attention. With a confident yet gentle demeanor, she prepared to share her heartfelt words with those gathered in the gymnasium.

"In the shadows of fear, a hero emerged,
A figure of strength when the world blurred.
With courage unyielding, he stood tall,
To shield me from harm, to break my fall.
In the chaos of the moment, his voice rang clear,
Guiding me through the darkness, calming my fear.
With selfless grace, he risked it all,
To answer the desperate, silent call.
So here I stand, with words to impart,
A gratitude deep, from the depths of my heart.
For you, dear savior, I owe my all,
For answering my plea, for breaking my fall.
Thank you, brave guardian, for your sacrifice,
For offering refuge, for paying the price.
In your shadow, I found light anew,
Forever grateful, forever true."

As Emily finished reciting her poem, the audience was silent, moved by the raw emotion and heartfelt gratitude woven into her words.

The sincerity in her voice, the raw emotion woven into every line, touched him deeply. He felt a lump form in his throat as he listened, his heart swelling with gratitude and humility.

Each word of appreciation, each expression of thanks, resonated with him, reminding him of the profound impact that one moment had on both their lives. In that moment, amidst the echo of her poetry, Sam felt a sense of validation, a reaffirmation of the importance of his role as a protector, a guardian of his community.

He couldn't help but feel overwhelmed by the magnitude of her gratitude, humbled by the realization of how profoundly his actions had touched her life.

As the talent show came to an end Sam stood up out of his chair. Being there and hearing those words made everything he went through worth it.

As he looked around he saw Emily walking towards him with someone that looked to be her mother.

Emily and her mother approached Sam, their faces alight with gratitude and sincerity. They expressed their heartfelt thanks for his bravery and quick thinking, for stepping in to protect her when she needed it most. Sam felt a swell of emotion as he looked at them, overwhelmed by their genuine appreciation.

He assured them that he was just doing his job, but their words touched him deeply nonetheless. As they exchanged a few more words, Sam couldn't help but feel a profound sense of connection with Emily and her mother, grateful for the opportunity to see firsthand the impact of his actions on their lives.

Walking away from the school, Sam couldn't shake the sense of amazement that lingered within him. The unexpected encounter with Emily at the talent show had been a pleasant surprise, a reminder of the ripple effects of his actions.

As he reflected on the events of the evening, Sam couldn't help but feel a renewed sense of purpose and fulfillment, knowing that he had made a difference in Emily's life.

It was a moment he wouldn't soon forget, a reminder of the profound impact that even the smallest acts of courage and kindness could have on others. With a sense of gratitude and contentment, Sam continued on his way, feeling more inspired and uplifted than ever before.

Sam's first day back on duty seemed to breeze by, buoyed by the overwhelming support and respect from the townspeople who now viewed him as a hero. The incident had not only reaffirmed the community's trust in its police force but also served as a powerful reminder of the town's resilience and unity in the face of adversity.

Chapter 15
Finding Peace

AS THE SUN BEGAN ITS descent, crickets singing in the warm Georgia air, Sam and Natalie met at their usual spot near the ice cream shop. The air was crisp and cool, carrying with it the faint scent of freshly cut grass and blooming flowers. A gentle breeze rustled through the trees, their leaves shimmering in the soft light of dusk.

The town square was relatively quiet, the sounds of birds chirping and distant laughter from children playing on the town square providing a serene backdrop to their conversation. The occasional car passed by on the nearby road, its headlights casting long shadows across the pavement.

Sam and Natalie strolled along the walkways, their footsteps echoing softly in the tranquil evening air. They exchanged easy conversation, their voices blending harmoniously with the sounds of nature around them. The sky above was painted in hues of orange and pink, the last remnants of daylight giving way to the velvety embrace of night.

As they walked, Sam and Natalie took in the sights and sounds of their small town, savoring the quiet beauty of the moment. With each step, they felt a sense of peace and contentment wash over them, knowing that they were exactly where they were meant to be, together, in this idyllic setting as the day drew to a close.

Seated on a weathered bench beneath the spreading branches of an ancient oak tree, Sam and Natalie found themselves immersed in a reflective conversation, their thoughts drifting back to the journey that had brought them to this moment.

"Do you remember the first time we met?" Natalie asked, a smile playing at the corners of her lips.

Sam had a nostalgic expression crossing his face. "Of course I do. It was at the cemetery."

Natalie chuckled softly, the memory clear in her mind. "I was so surprised to see someone else there besides us. I thought my family were the only ones who found solace among the gravestones."

"I felt the same way. It's a peaceful spot, away from the noise of the town."

"And yet, we found each other there," Natalie mused, a hint of wonder in her voice. "It's funny how life works sometimes."

Sam smiled, his eyes meeting hers with a fondness that spoke volumes. "Funny and unexpected. But I'm grateful for that moment. It led to so much more."

Natalie's gaze softened, filled with warmth and appreciation. "Me too. I never could have imagined that meeting you would change my life in such profound ways."

Sam reached out and gently took her hand in his, a silent gesture of solidarity and understanding. "Likewise. You've brought so much light into my life, Natalie."

Natalie's heart swelled with affection as she squeezed his hand gently. "And you've brought strength and courage into mine, Sam. I'll always be thankful for that."

"You've been my rock through all of this," Sam said, his voice filled with gratitude as he looked at Natalie.

Natalie smiled warmly, her eyes reflecting his sentiment. "I'm just glad I could be there for you, Sam. It's what friends are for."

"But you've been more than just a friend. You've been a source of strength and comfort when I needed it most." He responded.

Natalie's gaze softened, touched by his words. "I'm honored to have been able to support you, Sam. You've faced some tough challenges, and I admire your resilience."

Sam chuckled softly, a hint of self-deprecation in his tone. "I don't know if I would've made it through without you, Natalie. You kept me grounded when everything else felt like it was falling apart."

Natalie reached out and placed a hand on his arm, a gesture of solidarity and affection. "We've been through a lot together, Sam. And I wouldn't have it any other way."

"It's been quite a journey, hasn't it?" Sam mused, breaking the peaceful silence between them.

Natalie's gaze was thoughtful as she considered his words. "Definitely. And it's not over yet."

Sam smiled, his eyes reflecting determination. "No, it's just the beginning. We've faced some tough challenges, especially with everything going on in our town."

Natalie sighed, her expression tinged with sadness. "Race relations have always been a struggle here. But I believe we can make a difference, Sam."

"I do too. We've seen progress, especially with the recent events. Mayor Carter's statement about the police department protecting everyone regardless of race was a step in the right direction." He said in agreement.

Natalie's eyes sparkled with hope. "Exactly. And I think we can continue that momentum. We just have to keep working together, advocating for equality and justice."

Sam reached out and squeezed her hand, a silent affirmation of their shared goals. "I'm with you every step of the way, Natalie. Together, we can make a difference."

"Natalie," he continued, his voice trembling slightly, "there's something I've been wanting to ask you."

Natalie turned to him, her eyes curious but gentle. "What is it, Sam?"

Sam took a deep breath, his gaze meeting hers. "I know we've been friends for a while now, and... well, I've been thinking a lot about us. About what could be."

Natalie's brows furrowed in slight confusion, but she remained attentive, waiting for him to continue.

Sam's voice softened as he spoke, his vulnerability shining through. "Natalie, I care about you deeply. More than just a friend. And... I was wondering if you could ever see us being more than that. If you could see yourself... being my girlfriend?"

Natalie's breath caught in her throat, her heart skipping a beat at his words. She looked at Sam, her eyes shimmering with emotion. "Sam... are you asking me to be your girlfriend?"

Sam's gaze was unwavering. "Yes, Natalie. I am."

A soft smile tugged at the corners of Natalie's lips as she reached out to take Sam's hand in hers. "Then yes, Sam. Yes, I would love to be your girlfriend."

Sam felt a rush of relief and joy wash over him as he squeezed her hand gently, overcome with emotion. "Thank you, Natalie. You have no idea how much that means to me."

Natalie leaned in closer, her voice barely above a whisper. "I know it won't be easy, especially with everything going on. But I believe in us, Sam. I believe we're perfect together."

Tears tried their best to show up in Sam's eyes as he pulled her into a tight embrace, his heart overflowing with love and gratitude. "I believe it too, Natalie. And I promise to do everything I can to make this work. To make us work."

As they rose from the bench, a gentle breeze swept through, carrying with it a sense of closure and tranquility. Sam and Natalie shared a lingering embrace, holding onto each other as if they were afraid to let go. There was an unspoken understanding between them, a silent vow to stand by each other through thick and thin.

Their hug spoke volumes, conveying a depth of emotion that words could not capture. It was a moment of solace, a reassurance that no matter what challenges lay ahead, they would face them together, hand in hand.

As they finally pulled away, their eyes met, shimmering with unshed tears and a shared sense of resolve. With a tender smile, Sam brushed a stray strand of hair from Natalie's face, his touch gentle yet reassuring.

And then, in a moment that seemed to stretch on for eternity, they shared a kiss—a sweet, lingering exchange of love and affection. It was a testament to the bond they shared, a promise of unwavering devotion and support.

As Sam walked home, a sense of contentment settled over him like a warm blanket on a cool evening. The weight of the day's events, the highs and lows, seemed to lift from his shoulders, replaced by a feeling of fulfillment and peace.

With each step, he reflected on how far he had come since the beginning of his journey. From the challenges of his work to the unexpected twists and turns of fate, he had weathered it all with resilience and determination. And through it all, he had discovered a strength within himself that he never knew he had.

As he approached his front door, he paused for a moment, taking in the familiar sights and sounds of his neighborhood. The chirping of crickets, the soft glow of streetlights casting long shadows on the pavement—it was a scene that had become like a second home to him.

With a smile on his face, Sam unlocked the door and stepped inside, greeted by the warmth of his family's embrace. In that moment, surrounded by the love and support of those closest to him, he knew that he was not alone. Whatever challenges lay ahead, he would face them head-on, armed with the knowledge that he had the strength and resilience to overcome them.

As he settled in for the night, a sense of peace washed over him, lulling him into a restful sleep. Tomorrow was a new day, filled with endless possibilities and opportunities for growth. And as he drifted off into dreams, Sam knew that he was ready to embrace whatever the future had in store, secure in the knowledge that he was exactly where he was meant to be.

As the sun dipped below the horizon, casting long shadows across the quiet town of Pineworth, Sam watched Natalie disappear around the corner, her presence lingering in his mind long after she was gone. Lost in thought, he rounded another corner and almost collided with Chief Johnson, who was making his way down the sidewalk with purposeful strides.

"Sorry about that, Chief," Sam said, stepping aside to let him pass.

"No worries, Sam," Chief Johnson replied, his voice carrying a hint of weariness. "Just lost in thought, I suppose."

Sam nodded in understanding, falling into step beside the Chief as they walked.

"I've been meaning to talk to you. About the state of the town."

Sam's interest was piqued. He knew that the recent incidents had left their mark on Pineworth, and he was eager to hear the Chief's perspective.

"What's on your mind, Chief?" Sam inquired, his tone tinged with curiosity.

Chief Johnson clasped his hands behind his back, adopting a thoughtful stance. "I've been keeping a close eye on things, Sam. And I have to say, despite the challenges we've faced, I'm optimistic about the direction we're heading."

Sam listened intently, his attention fully focused on the Chief's words. He had always respected Chief Johnson's insights and valued his guidance.

"We've come through some tough times," the Chief continued, his voice steady. "But your actions, and those of your fellow officers, have shown the strength of our community. We're resilient, Sam. And we're stronger together."

Sam felt a swell of pride at the Chief's words. It was a validation of everything he believed in, a reaffirmation of the importance of their work as law enforcement officers.

"I couldn't agree more, Chief," Sam replied, a sense of determination shining in his eyes. "I'm proud to serve this town, and I'll do whatever it takes to keep it safe."

Chief Johnson shook his head approvingly, a hint of a smile playing at the corners of his lips. "I know you will, Sam. And I have every confidence that together, we'll continue to make Pineworth a place we can all be proud of."

With that, they exchanged a firm handshake, their shared commitment to the town and its people binding them together in purpose.

As Sam strolled through the town square, a gentle breeze rustled through the trees, carrying with it the first hint of autumn. The air was crisp and invigorating, a welcome change from the oppressive heat of summer. It was the kind of day that made you want to linger outside, to soak in the tranquility of the moment.

Sam found himself lost in thought as he walked, the events of the past weeks playing out in his mind like scenes from a movie. From the tension of the school protest to the harrowing encounter with the gunman, it had been a rollercoaster of emotions, a test of resilience and courage.

As he reflected on everything that had transpired, Sam couldn't help but feel a sense of awe at the resilience of his community. Despite the challenges they had faced, they had come together, united in their determination to overcome adversity and build a better future for themselves and their children.

"I never thought I'd see the day," Sam mused aloud, his voice carried away in the breeze. "But here we are, stronger than ever."

He paused, taking a moment to appreciate the beauty of the town square, the familiar sights and sounds that had been a constant throughout his life. It was a reminder of the resilience of the human spirit, of the capacity to rise above adversity and find peace in the midst of chaos.

"I guess sometimes it takes a crisis to bring out the best in people," Sam continued, his thoughts turning introspective. "But I'm grateful for it. Grateful for the lessons learned, the bonds forged, and the strength discovered within ourselves."

He fell silent then, allowing the stillness of the moment to wash over him, a sense of peace settling in his heart. For in that moment, surrounded by the beauty of his hometown and the warmth of its people, Sam knew that no matter what the future held, he would face it with courage and conviction, secure in the knowledge that he was exactly where he was meant to be.

As Sam's car eased into the driveway, he spotted his mother sitting on the porch, bathed in the soft glow of the setting sun. The sight of her brought a sense of warmth and comfort, like coming home after a long journey.

"Hey, Mom," Sam greeted her as he stepped out of the car, the gravel crunching beneath his shoes. "Beautiful evening, isn't it?"

His mother turned to him, a gentle smile gracing her lips. "Sure is, Sam. How was your day?"

Sam settled into the chair beside her, taking a moment to gather his thoughts. "It was good, Mom. Eventful, as always."

His mother looked at him, her gaze thoughtful. "I heard about what happened at the talent show. You must be proud of yourself."

Sam shrugged, a modest smile playing at the corners of his lips. "I guess so. It was unexpected, that's for sure."

They sat in comfortable silence for a moment, the only sound the chirping of crickets in the distance. Then, Sam took a deep breath, steeling himself for what he was about to say.

"Mom, there's something I need to tell you," he began, his voice steady. "I'm going to be seeing Natalie."

His mother's eyes widened in surprise, but there was a warmth in her expression that put Sam at ease.

"Really?" she said, her voice tinged with curiosity.

He spoke of Natalie's kindness, her strength, and her unwavering support throughout the recent challenges they had faced. He spoke of the connection they shared, the way she made him feel alive and hopeful for the future.

His mother listened intently, her gaze softening with each word. When Sam had finished, she reached out and took his hand in hers, a silent gesture of love and understanding.

"I'm so proud of you, Sam," she said, her voice barely above a whisper. "You've grown into a remarkable young man, one who sees the potential for change and isn't afraid to fight for it. Natalie is a wonderful girl, and I'm happy to hear that you've found happiness with her."

Sam felt a lump form in his throat, the weight of his mother's words washing over him like a wave. In that moment, he knew that no matter what challenges lay ahead, he would always have his mother's love and support to guide him.

"Thanks, Mom," he said, his voice thick with emotion. "I love you."

"I love you too, Sam," his mother replied, pulling him into a tight embrace. And as they sat there together, bathed in the golden light of the evening sun, Sam felt a profound sense of gratitude for the bond they shared,and for the journey that had brought them to this moment of peace and understanding.

As the sun dipped below the horizon, casting the sky in hues of pink and gold, Sam felt a sense of calm wash over him. He stood on the porch with his mother, their silhouettes framed against the fading light, and he knew that this moment would stay with him forever.

In that quiet moment, surrounded by the familiar sights and sounds of home, Sam realized that he had found peace. Peace in his job, knowing that he was making a difference in his community. Peace in his relationships, knowing that he had friends and loved ones who supported him unconditionally. And most importantly, peace within himself, knowing that he was exactly where he was meant to be.

As he looked out at the world stretching out before him, Sam felt a sense of gratitude for the journey that had brought him to this point. The challenges, the triumphs, the moments of doubt and uncertainty—all of it had shaped him into the person he is today.

And as he turned to his mother, a smile playing at the corners of his lips, he knew that no matter what the future held, he would face it with courage and determination, for he had learned that true strength came not from the absence of fear, but from the willingness to confront it head-on.

With a final glance at the sky, Sam took his mother's hand in his and squeezed it gently.

Together, they stepped back into the warmth of their home, ready to embrace whatever adventures lay ahead.

And as the stars began to twinkle overhead, casting their soft glow upon the world below, Sam knew that he was exactly where he was meant to be—right here, right now, in this moment of perfect peace.

Epilogue

In the weeks and months that followed, life in Pineworth settled back into a sense of normalcy. The town, once rocked by the events surrounding the school protest and the shooting incident, began to heal, its wounds mending with each passing day. And amidst the backdrop of a changing world, Sam Anderson's journey continued, marked by moments of triumph, growth, and love.

As Sam returned to his duties as a police officer, he found himself met with newfound respect and admiration from his fellow townsfolk. The events of that fateful day had solidified his place as a hero in the eyes of many, but for Sam, the true reward lay in knowing that he had made a difference—that his actions had helped to bring about positive change in his community.

With each passing day, Sam's bond with Natalie grew stronger, tand heir relationship blossoming into something beautiful and enduring. Together, they navigated the challenges of race relations and societal expectations, finding solace and strength in each other's love and support. And as they stood side by side, facing the uncertainties of the future, they knew that together, they could overcome anything that came their way.

In the months that followed, Sam continued to excel in his role as a police officer, earning the respect and admiration of his peers and the community at large. His leadership and dedication were recognized by Chief Johnson, who soon promoted him to the rank of Sergeant—a testament to Sam's unwavering commitment to serving and protecting the people of Pineworth.

Meanwhile, Natalie's career as a nurse flourished, her passion for helping others driving her to new heights of success and fulfillment.

Together, she and Sam became a beacon of hope and inspiration in their community, their love story serving as a reminder that in the face of adversity, love and unity could prevail.

And as the years passed, Sam and Natalie's love endured, their bond growing stronger with each passing day. Together, they faced life's challenges with courage and resilience, their love serving as a guiding light through even the darkest of times.

In the end, Sam's journey was not just one of personal growth and triumph, but of love, friendship, and the enduring power of the human spirit. And as he looked back on the twists and turns of his life's path, he knew that every step had led him exactly where he was meant to be—home, in the arms of the woman he loved, surrounded by the warmth and love of his community.

As the sun set on another day in Pineworth, Sam smiled, knowing that his journey was far from over—that the best was yet to come.

And so, with hope in his heart and a sense of purpose in his soul, he embraced the journey that lay ahead, ready to face whatever challenges and adventures awaited him, secure in the knowledge that he was exactly where he was meant to be.

Don't miss out!

Visit the website below and you can sign up to receive emails whenever K.E.W. publishes a new book. There's no charge and no obligation.

https://books2read.com/r/B-A-RJUBB-UIFJD

BOOKS2READ

Connecting independent readers to independent writers.

Did you love *1971*? Then you should read *Secrets Among The Stones*[1] by K.E.W.!

[2]

"Secrets Among The Stones", the reviting 4th book in "The Pineworth Chronicles" series, is a story set in the small town of Pineworth. Detective Alex Bennett gets caught up in a complicated situation involving secrets, lies, and a murder. After a well-known resident named Henry Winters is discovered dead, the once-peaceful town is thrown into chaos.

The story takes unexpected turns as Alex follows leads and uncovers hidden connections while navigating the complexities of small-town dynamics. With each chapter, the tension rises, culminating in a thrilling chase, a surprising arrest, and a revelation that shakes the town to its core.

---

1. https://books2read.com/u/3L5yW5

2. https://books2read.com/u/3L5yW5

It is a compelling mystery novel that combines suspense, intrigue, and a touch of small-town charm. It weaves elements of detective work, family drama, and historical mysteries, creating a captivating tale that keeps readers on the edge of their seats until the end.

Read more at https://www.instagram.com/whitequillwritings/.

Also by K.E.W.

The Pineworth Chronicles
Secrets Among The Stones
1971

Standalone
The Pineworth Chronicles
Room Below The World
School Safety Pocket Handbook
A Walk Among Soldiers
Confessions Of The Lost

Watch for more at https://www.instagram.com/whitequillwritings/.

About the Author

K.E.W. is a storyteller devoted to exploring the fragile spaces between history, memory, and imagination. Blending meticulous research with a deep sense of humanity, their works span historical fiction, small-town dramas, and haunting psychological tales. Through each book, K.E.W. seeks to capture the resilience of ordinary people living through extraordinary times, while inviting readers to reflect on their own connections to family, community, and the past.

Read more at https://www.instagram.com/whitequillwritings/.

About the Publisher

White Quill Writings was founded in 2023 on the shared passion for storytelling and literary expression, White Quill Writings is the brainchild of a devoted husband and wife duo. With a vision to empower authors and bring exceptional stories to life, they embarked on this self-publishing venture.

Driven by a commitment to support emerging voices and diverse narratives, White Quill Writings offers a platform that values creativity, authenticity, and individuality. Their dedication to nurturing writers shines through personalized guidance, professional editing, and tailored publishing solutions.

As a testament to their unwavering belief in the power of words, this partnership fosters a community where stories flourish, authors thrive, and dreams of publication become tangible realities. White Quill Writings stands as an inviting gateway for writers seeking to share their unique tales with the world.

Read more at https://instagram.com/whitequillwritings.